"I should've taken you straight to the Sundance."

Hannah gaped at him. "No way. And miss this?"

"Don't worry. In a week you'll see your fill of stars."

"That's not what I meant," Hannah said.

Seth cupped her face with one hand and deepened the kiss, their tongues touching and stroking each other. His hand moved to her neckline, and he toyed with the fabric before dipping his fingers just underneath, just enough to tease.

She trembled when his mouth left hers and his lips blazed a damp path down the side of her neck.

The temptation was there. She could feel his tension, his indecision, his restraint.

Oh, God, how she wanted to touch him. But she didn't dare. His mouth was hot and hungry, his skin feverish. His warm, rugged scent surrounded her. It was all going to her head.

Stepping just one toe over the line would be all it took. They wouldn't stop.

And there would be no turning back...

Dear Reader,

I'm happy to say Blackfoot Falls, a kissing cousin to the Rocky Mountains, is still alive and kicking, and waiting for you to pay a visit. In this story you'll be bumping into quite a few characters you already know from the Sundance and Whispering Pines ranches, as well as a handful of townsfolk who keep the rumor mill well-oiled. To add to the fun and mayhem, you'll also meet a new troublemaker who's mixing it up with the old ones.

After writing sixteen books set in Blackfoot Falls, it's amazing how attached I've become to the town and its cast of characters. Although some of them would tell you otherwise and they'd have a point. When I started writing someone we haven't seen in a while, I got annoyed with myself. How could I have left Barbara McAllister on the sidelines for so long? Completely unforgivable!

And then we have the hero and heroine—Seth and Hannah. I generally form bonds with all my characters, though on many different levels. When Hannah met Seth, I knew these two were destined for a happy-ever-after, and no interference from me would change their destiny. Not that I wanted to keep them apart. I can honestly say that at the end of the book, I felt as though I was saying goodbye to two very good friends. I didn't want them to leave. But of course they'll be with me for a while...making me smile.

I hope they make you smile, as well.

Regards,

Debbi Rawlins

Debbi Rawlins

Sizzling Summer Nights

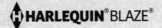

Recycling programs
for this product may
not exist in your area.

ISBN-13: 978-0-373-79957-2

Sizzling Summer Nights

Copyright © 2017 by Debbi Quattrone

Printed in U.S.A.

Debbi Rawlins grew up in the country and loves Western movies and books. Her first crush was on a cowboy—okay, he was an actor in the role of a cowboy, but she was only eleven, so it counts. It was Houston, Texas, where she first started writing for Harlequin, and now she has her own ranch...of sorts. Instead of horses, she has four dogs, four cats, a trio of goats and free-range cattle on a few acres in gorgeous rural Utah.

Books by Debbi Rawlins

Harlequin Blaze

Made in Montana

Barefoot Blue Jean Night
Own the Night
On a Snowy Christmas Night
You're Still the One
No One Needs to Know
From This Moment On
Alone with You
Need You Now
Behind Closed Doors
Anywhere with You
Come On Over
This Kiss
Come Closer, Cowboy
Wild for You
Hot Winter Nights

To get the inside scoop on Harlequin Blaze and its talented writers, visit Facebook.com/BlazeAuthors.

All backlist available in ebook format.

Visit the Author Profile page
at Harlequin.com for more titles.

This is for my editor, Laura Barth, who's been with me for the whole series, through thick and thin, for better or for worse, and for *Oh, my God, I'm never going to finish this book!*

And please, no one tell her, but Hannah is a little like Laura in some ways. That's all I'm saying.

Thanks also to Jo Leigh, my partner in crime and plotting.

1

"I've stayed out of trouble for six years," Hannah Hastings said, shaking her head, resigned and not nearly tipsy enough. "And now you're going to make me do this, aren't you?"

"Of course I am." Rachel grinned at her. "Get up there before someone beats you to the mic."

"Gee, that would be a shame." Sighing, Hannah pushed back in the old oak chair. "No pictures."

"Yeah, right. Okay."

"I mean it. Put your damn phone away. We're not stupid college kids anymore."

"No?" Rachel burst out laughing.

"I haven't taken a vacation in four years," Hannah muttered. "And I decide to come all the way to Montana to see you. I'm such an idiot." She drained the last of her watered-down margarita, then got to her feet, glaring at the small makeshift stage next to the jukebox. "What's wrong with you people? Who does karaoke night anymore?"

She glanced around at the good-sized crowd crammed into the rustic bar. The Watering Hole was supposed to be a nice, quiet place where they could talk, catch up with what had been happening to each other since their college days. Ha.

Tears from laughing filled Rachel's eyes. Sitting next to her, Jamie, her sister-in-law, only had a vague idea of what was going on but it seemed that laughter really was contagious.

God help her. Hannah figured she might as well get it over with. She just wished this wasn't her first night in Blackfoot Falls. She'd only be here a week. Not nearly long enough for these nice people to forgive and forget.

Now, the tall, dark-haired cowboy sitting at the bar? He was the one she really cared about. Since walking in five minutes ago he'd kept his head down and nursed his beer. Bad break-up was Hannah's guess. Poor guy showed all the signs of love gone wrong. Something she might've been willing to help him forget for a while. But what were the odds he wouldn't turn around to see who couldn't carry a tune with both hands and a two-ton pickup truck?

Oh, and who had the nerve to get up in front of a roomful of strangers and completely humiliate herself. Sure, he'd be all over her. She wouldn't be able to fight him off.

Five stupid minutes. Rachel couldn't have called in her marker before then?

Hannah sat down again. "Is there an expiration date on that coupon? I bet there is."

Rachel grinned. "Nope."

"Let me see it." Hannah stuck her hand out, wiggling her fingers. "Not that I don't trust you."

"I'm not giving you this piece of paper. You'll probably swallow it."

Hannah sighed. "Jamie, would you mind checking? And make sure it isn't Rachel's handwriting."

"Wow, she really doesn't trust you," Jamie said, grinning, as she leaned over for a look. "Sorry. I think it's legit. Says it was for her twenty-second birthday?"

"Okay, who holds on to something like that for six years? That's just sick." Most of the women in their sorority had been too broke to afford gifts, so they'd gotten creative with coupons. Everyone had cashed them in right away. No one would've thought to include an expiration date.

"Better get up there before I feel inclined to make an announcement," Rachel said sweetly.

Hannah hesitated. She had an idea that just might work. "Rachel...listen, you know I'm always up for a challenge, but there's a guy in here that I—"

"Who?" Rachel sat up straighter. "Where?"

With a pitying look, Jamie shook her head at Hannah. "Are you nuts?"

"She's still that bad, huh?"

Jamie nodded and signaled for their waitress.

Apparently marriage hadn't tempered Rachel's annoying hobby of trying to fix up her single friends. If Hannah had stopped to think about it, she probably would've realized that the gold band on Rachel's finger could never curb her enthusiasm, but only make it worse.

Lord, it was hard to believe Rachel was married. Doing her dad a favor had prevented Hannah from attending the wedding. She hated that she'd missed it. And for what? She was no closer to pleasing the old man than on the day she'd been born the wrong gender. It was a lost cause.

Ignoring them, Rachel surveyed the bar like a hawk circling its next meal. "Just tell me who he is and I might let you off the hook."

"I'll take my chances." Hannah purposely didn't look in his direction.

With that damn uncanny ability of hers, Rachel whipped her gaze around and hit a bull's-eye. "Seth Landers?" she asked. "Because you'd like him. Nice guy. Has some issues. Nothing horrible. Just enough to make him interesting."

"I don't know who you're talking about. And just so we're clear, I'm not doing a whole song." Hannah took a couple of steps, and stopped. "Jamie, please tell the waitress to make my margarita full octane this time."

"You got it," Jamie said, and laughed when Hannah made it another foot and stopped again.

"It's going to get bad, so if you want to step outside for a few minutes, you won't hurt my feelings."

"And miss everyone's reaction?" Rachel said. "Not a chance."

"I think I'm already missing something." Jamie's puzzled frown was aimed at Rachel. "You look positively evil right now."

"Don't worry about Hannah. She's fearless. Just wait."

Hannah tried not to look in Seth's direction. Luckily, his mug of beer seemed to be the only thing that interested him.

A perky little blonde finished her rendition of *Need You Now*, curtsied to the hooting and applause and left the small stage.

Hannah decided she needed this to be over with and hurried to pick up the mic. The song she selected was an oldie. She'd given up karaoke nights right after college and didn't know which tunes were the current faves. Although, in her case, it really didn't matter.

She rubbed a sweaty palm down the front of her jeans.

Maybe she should just admit to Rachel that she wasn't the same daring person she'd been in school. What good was pride if she ended up dying from embarrassment?

On the other hand, maybe this was just what she needed to loosen up. What the hell, she didn't know anyone here. Except Rachel. And now Jamie. Ah, and Nikki, sister-in-law number two, who happened to be the bartender at the moment. She was talking to Seth. Sure would be swell if she kept him distracted until Hannah finished making a fool of herself.

The music started. Hannah knew all the words to the song but she kept her eyes on the small monitor and started singing her heart out. It felt pretty good, just like the old days. Before she'd discovered that getting through college was the easiest part of life.

The guys playing pool in the back room left their game to stare at her. Even the waitress, carrying a full tray of drinks, had stopped between tables. People sitting with their backs to her twisted around in their seats, probably afraid it was a disaster drill. Hannah used to get that one a lot.

She refused to look at Rachel, though, or the cowboy. Heaven forbid, she might get nervous and start singing on key.

After the longest three minutes of her life, and likely everyone else's in the bar, Hannah set down the mic. A brief crackle of static pierced the shocked silence.

Oh, what the hell.

She took a bow.

Laughter and applause broke out. She even heard some boot stompin', courtesy of two pool players. God bless cowboys. She'd never cared for them before but might have to rethink her position.

Head held high, she walked back to the table and sat down, facing Rachel. "Happy?"

"You have no idea." Her cheeks were almost the color of her auburn hair.

Hannah risked a peek at Seth. Huh. Had he turned around at all?

"Lady, you've got guts." Jamie slid the fresh margarita across the table. "This is on me."

"Thanks." Hannah took a quick sip, realizing she should've asked for water, too. "Can you believe she made me do that?"

"Oh, please." Rachel dabbed at her eyes. "Like you haven't dragged me over the coals plenty of times."

"Me? I would never!" The three of them laughed, then Hannah glanced over her shoulder at the pool tables. "Is there only one waitress?"

"I don't know," Rachel said. "What do you need?"

"Just some water." Hannah rose, feeling a bit wobbly. Not from booze. She hadn't drunk much. "Either of you want anything?"

Rachel's cell beeped. "I'm good," she said, her gaze on the phone.

Jamie shook her head. "Hey, ask Nikki if she's closing tonight, would you?"

"Sure." Hannah wove her way around the tables, grinning at the good-natured remarks about her performance, and headed toward Nikki, who was wiping down the bar near Seth.

"That was...pretty damn awesome," she said with a laugh. "Had to be Rachel who got you up there."

"Of course it was." Hannah rolled her eyes. "I hope I didn't chase away any customers."

"Are you kidding? Everyone loved it."

"Or they're all in shock."

Still laughing, Nikki tossed the rag. "Want another margarita? I'm buying."

"No, thanks. Water would be great, though."

Hannah couldn't tell if Seth had even bothered to look

up. Resisting the urge to check him out, she focused on Nikki's glossy dark hair as she bent to open the small fridge. They'd met earlier at the Sundance just after Hannah had arrived at the ranch. Nikki was married to Rachel's brother, Trace. Which reminded Hannah to chew out her so-called friend. Back in their sorority days everyone knew Rachel had brothers, but had she ever mentioned they were all hotties? And now all three were married.

Nikki straightened and uncapped the bottle. "Anything else?"

"Oh, yes, Jamie wants to know if you're closing tonight."

"Afraid so," Nikki said, and set the water on the bar.

Thirsty from nervous dry mouth, Hannah reached for the bottle.

"How late do you stay open on weekends?" Seth's voice was deep, gravelly and unexpected.

Hannah knocked the bottle over. Water shot out and splashed her on the chin before spilling across the scarred wood and down the front of her jeans. She and Nikki both went for the bottle. Nikki was quicker.

Luckily, Hannah wasn't too wet and she didn't think any of the spray had reached Seth.

She turned and met his hazel eyes. "Did I get you?"

"Nope." He ran his gaze down the front of her blouse to her jeans and lingered on her hips. "You don't look too bad."

For a second she wondered how to take that, then got caught up studying his strong, unshaven jaw and the deep cleft in his chin. His lips were pulled into a thin line, and she realized he was fighting a smile. He had thick lashes as dark as his collar-length hair. He must've been wearing a hat earlier. It had left a ridge.

She hoped it was a Stetson.

"Oh…" She met those heart-melting eyes again. "It's my turn to talk, isn't it?"

SETH LANDERS HAD been wondering how he should go about getting laid tonight. Generally it wasn't a problem for him. His luck ran better than most if anyone listened to the guys in the bunkhouse. The trick was finding a nice, willing woman here in town, someone who wasn't a local so he'd be less likely to get himself in any trouble. That being his number one goal these days, he'd suffer through a few more weeks of abstinence if he absolutely had to. Hell, he hoped not.

"I'm Hannah." She extended a slim hand that was still damp from the spill. Her skin was soft, pale, and she had a slight southern accent. Texas maybe. Her inflection reminded him of his old air force buddy from Houston.

"Seth Landers."

"I know. I mean…" She glanced back at her table. "Rachel mentioned it. Rachel McAllister… Gunderson, actually."

"Ah. She say anything else?"

"Hmm. Not that I recall." Her gaze went to Nikki. "Do you have something I can use on the floor? A rag maybe?"

"Should I get the mop?"

"No, it's just an itty-bitty spot, but someone could slip," Hannah said, staring at her feet.

She was pretty. Brown eyes, brown hair, a heart-shaped face, nothing that stood out. But pretty all the same. Nice smile. Yeah, she had a real nice smile. If she weren't drunk and a friend of Rachel's, he would've gone for her.

The minute he walked in he'd pegged her as a guest at

the Sundance. Before he'd moved back to help his brother run their family ranch, Seth had heard the McAllisters had opened a dude ranch separate from their cattle operation. What he hadn't known was that their guests were mostly twenty-something women, a good many of them looking for vacation flings.

A couple of hired men had been scoring left and right, but Paxton and Joe had made a deal not to clue Seth in on their little gold mine. Then last week Joe had let it slip. Dumb greedy bastards. Seth had threatened them with a month of flood irrigation duty, a chore that made for endlessly long days. That would teach them. They'd be too damn tired to dip their buckets in anybody's well.

He smiled thinking about the looks on their faces, even though they knew he never would've done anything like that. Guess it was easy for them to forget he was their boss. Up until seven months ago, he hadn't been around all that much.

It bothered him to think about what a shit he'd been, sullen and uncommunicative, mad at the world and leaving the responsibility of the Whispering Pines to his dad and brother. Clint had suffered the brunt of it. But Seth was here to stay, making it up to his brother, hell, his whole family, for as long as it took. He just needed to stay out of trouble and let time heal.

Rag in hand, Nikki started to come around the bar but stopped for a guy wanting his mug refilled.

"I'll get it, Nikki." Seth reached across the bar.

"No," Hannah said, trying to snatch the rag from him. "It was my fault. I'll do it."

He got off the stool, and when she stubbornly refused to move, he crouched down right in front of her, putting his face level with her crotch.

Not a wise move. His thoughts shot in every direction

but the right one, while his body reacted as if he'd never been with a woman before. For Christ's sake, it wasn't as if he could see anything.

It seemed he'd mopped half the floor before he finally trusted himself to stand.

Hannah hadn't moved, other than to place both hands on her slim, curvy hips and frown at him.

"You're welcome," he said, and dropped the rag into Nikki's outstretched hand.

"Thank you." Hannah inched back and came up against a stool.

He hadn't meant to crowd her. He quickly got out of her way and returned to his seat.

She had a pleasant scent, nothing floral or cloying. Maybe it was just her. Seth normally didn't care for perfumes of any kind. Even her breath smelled nice, no hint of booze. He'd heard her massacre that song, though. He wondered if she was that gutsy when she was sober.

He returned to his seat just as Nikki set another water on the bar.

"Here you go," she said to Hannah. "I'll let you open this one."

Hannah laughed. "God, you'd think I was drunk."

In mid-sip, Seth chuckled and nearly sprayed her. Wouldn't that have been a hell of a thing? He lowered the mug and wiped his mouth.

"Nice meeting you, Seth. And thanks again."

"Any time." He turned just enough to watch her walk back to the table without being obvious.

She had a nice backside view in those slim-fitting jeans. The heels on the snazzy boots made her look taller. By his estimate, without them, she was around five-six.

A few seconds after Hannah sat down, Rachel jumped

up. So did the blonde sitting with them, but she lingered with Hannah while Rachel approached the bar.

"Hey, Seth. How's the family?"

"Good. Working hard."

"I know what you mean," she said and motioned for Nikki, who nodded as she poured drinks at the other end. "We sure don't need any more of these scorching hot summers." Rachel shrugged. "Could be worse, I suppose. I pity the ranchers in Texas."

"Amen to that. How's the dude ranch business treating you?"

"The money's decent. And mostly it's been fun." Rachel grinned. "My brothers might tell you otherwise."

"I met Hannah," he said, as if Rachel and half the people in the joint hadn't noticed. "I assume she's a guest?"

"She's from Dallas and staying at the Sundance, although I invited her to stay with Matt and me. We're old college friends."

Nikki brought a foaming mug with her and set it in front of him.

"Ah, no, thanks. One's my limit. Unless you want to drive me home." He wasn't hitting on her. She knew it and just laughed.

Rachel's soft smile told him she recalled the trouble he'd gotten into years ago. Folks in this flyspeck town had long memories. Rachel wasn't judging, though, and he appreciated that.

"Your beer is warm and flat by now," Nikki said. "Just drink what you want and I'll pour out the rest."

"Listen, Nik," Rachel said. "I need to run up to Kalispell for Matt. He needs a part for the tractor by morning."

"What's the matter?" Nikki asked. "He can't get it himself?"

"He could, except I was supposed to pick it up yesterday, and I forgot. Just like he said I would. So, of course I'm not admitting to it. Anyway, I should be back before you close. If I'm not, can you give Hannah a lift to the Sundance?"

"You're leaving her here?" Seth said, before Nikki could answer or he had stopped to think.

Both women gave him strange looks. He was touchy about leaving someone who was drunk on their own. Nikki was a relative newcomer and wouldn't understand. But Rachel did. His own hang-up aside, it surprised him that she'd abandon her friend.

"Well, yeah, I can't imagine she'd like driving to a garage. She'll have more fun here. Even Jamie doesn't want to go. She's meeting Cole."

Hell, it was none of his business. He glanced over and saw a young cowboy hitting on her. Hannah was going to get plenty of that kind of attention. Could be what she wanted.

"I don't mind taking her," Nikki said. "But it'll be late, unless Sadie comes in and closes up."

"Like I said, I hope to be back by ten. Possibly elevenish." Rachel paused. "Seth? What's wrong?"

"Nothing," he muttered, dragging his gaze away from Hannah. Nah, he had to say something. "You really think it's a good idea to leave her here alone?"

"Um, she's twenty-eight. I'm pretty sure she can take care of herself."

"But she's drunk."

Rachel grinned. "No, she's not."

"Hell, I'm not judging." He glanced at Nikki. "You know I'd be the last one to do that."

"I get why you think she is," Rachel said, laughing. "She just can't sing."

Seth wasn't buying it. Nobody in their right mind would get on that stage and do what she did to that song.

"I hope you bring her back in before she leaves," Nikki said. "That was priceless."

"I'll admit, I called in a chit from our college days. She wasn't all that anxious to get up there. But she's fearless. I knew she'd do it."

A blonde waitress walked past them, waving an order ticket.

Seth didn't recognize her, but then he'd been gone most of the last ten years. She gave him a sassy smile, and he smiled back. But she had to be a local and he didn't want to go there, so he broke eye contact quickly. Too bad about Hannah being Rachel's friend.

"Kristen, same thing?" Nikki got a nod and grabbed the tequila from the back shelf. "Yeah, don't worry. I'll get Hannah to the Sundance," Nikki said, and started toward Kristen waiting at the end of the bar.

"Thanks," Rachel said. "Oh, Seth, how about you? If you're still around and Nikki has to close, any chance you can give Hannah a ride?"

He heard Nikki laugh, caught a brief glimpse of her giving Rachel an eye-roll. So maybe Hannah being a friend wasn't a problem at all. "Sure," he said. "Count on it."

2

NOT LONG AFTER Rachel left, Hannah took Seth up on his offer to drive her to the Sundance. She'd resisted at first, not wanting to impose, but it seemed he wasn't going to leave the bar without her. Once they were outside, he gestured to the right. "My truck's that way."

Hannah hesitated. "Tell me the truth," she said giving it a final try. "Did Rachel twist your arm? Because, honestly, I don't mind waiting for Nikki."

"Nah, I figured I'd play hero and rescue you from the masses."

She still wasn't sure she believed him, and she would've told him just that, if it weren't for that ridiculously charming smile of his. It was a tad crooked, the corner of his mouth hiking up slightly higher on one side. The adorably boyish look was an amazing contrast to the dark intensity of his eyes. "Those guys had to be pretty drunk to ask me for an encore."

Seth chuckled. "That's downtown Saturday night for you. Up ahead is the Full Moon Saloon. Been open almost a year now. Before that, we had only the one bar."

"Wow. The Watering Hole is kind of small, too."

"The Full Moon is supposed to be a lot bigger. I heard

they have live music some nights and a mechanical bull in the back."

"You haven't checked it out yet?"

He shook his head. "I'd been away for a while. I moved back seven months ago but I don't come to town much."

Hannah got the feeling he didn't really want to talk about himself so she held her curiosity at bay. Anyway, she could get all the information she wanted from Rachel. "Well, Montana is beautiful country, so green, and the mountains are breathtaking. I don't understand how you could've left in the first place."

"It won't be all that green for much longer. Not with the heat we've been having."

"Well, I'm from Dallas, and it's been exceptionally hot for a couple years now."

"Yeah, Rachel mentioned you're from there." He was over six feet tall, with long legs that could probably go much faster but he stayed at a nice comfortable pace that better suited her.

"I don't know if you've ever been to Texas, but excuse me for not being sympathetic when you say it won't be green much longer."

"I've been there," he said. "I seem to recall some nice areas."

"Of course there are, mostly in the Hill Country, but overall it's been so dry and just…brown and ugly."

"Yep, the drought has hurt a lot of folks—ranchers, farmers and ultimately the consumer." He gestured to a sign posted in the window of a bakery. "As a matter of fact, there's going to be a town meeting on the topic."

Hannah had been too busy looking at the bakery's name. The Cake Whisperer. Cute. She caught only a quick glimpse of the handwritten sign as they walked past it. "Grazing permits. What does that have to do with the drought?"

"Cattle have to eat," he said. "If you don't have enough grass on your own land, you have to find some. It just so happens the government owns a good deal of prime grazing land," Seth said, with an enigmatic smile that revealed nothing of his political leaning.

Something that Hannah understood. Discussions about politics and religion always made her edgy. "So, the local ranchers can get a permit and let their cows graze on government grass?"

"For a fee, yes. And not just local ranchers, some of whom have been using the land for decades without a permit. Hence, the *emergency* meeting. It's a touchy subject around here. That's why I stay out of it."

"Huh." She wondered if her father knew anything about grazing permits or had thought about looking beyond Texas. Depending on shipping costs, leasing land here could solve his problem. Maybe she'd poke around and get some info.

Right now, though, she was more interested in Seth. His language surprised her. With his scuffed boots, worn jeans and blue T-shirt, he looked like a typical cowboy. Sometimes he sounded like one, and other times not at all. Now she really wanted to grill Rachel about him. What had she said about him having issues?

"Ask me," he said with an air of amusement.

At the sudden realization she'd been staring, she blinked. "Ask you what?"

"Whatever it is that's got you thinking so hard."

Tempting, but no, she'd wait for Rachel. It was possible the night could end really well and she didn't want to mess things up. "Where did you park? The next county?"

Seth stopped and opened the passenger door of a late model, dark gray truck. "Here we go."

"Is this yours?"

"No, but it's closer," he said, pulling the door wide. "Go ahead. We're all friends here. We swap vehicles all the time."

Hannah opened her mouth to ask if he was joking, then closed it without a word.

He laughed. "Of course it's mine."

"I knew that," she said, glaring up at him.

Humor lit his eyes. He really was very good-looking and it was all she could do not to touch his dimpled chin.

Before she gave in to the impulse, she looked up at the June sky filled with stars. So many that she couldn't keep count if she tried.

"Sorry," she said, when it registered that he was waiting for her. "The sky is so beautiful out here."

"I couldn't agree more." His gaze swept the vast expanse of inky backdrop. "I've visited a lot of different places, and so far nothing beats a Montana sky. Probably why I loved astronomy so much as a kid."

"Really? Not anymore?"

"Ah, you know…" He shrugged. "Life happened."

"I get it. Oddly enough, I was just thinking about how stargazing had been one of my favorite things to do as a little girl. Now I can't remember the last time I slowed down long enough to look up."

"Did you grow up in Dallas?"

"No. My parents own a small ranch a couple hours west of the city in the middle of nowhere."

"A ranch?" His brows went up. "No kidding?"

Hannah wished she hadn't told him that part. He'd expect her to know things about ranching. But her father hadn't taught her anything, or wanted her around. He'd considered her a nuisance. "When I say small, that's not an exaggeration."

"But your folks raise cattle?" he asked, and she nodded. "How many head?"

"I'm guessing around a hundred. My dad works by himself."

"That's not as small as you think. Statistically speaking, fifty head is closer to the average. But, yep, he could easily handle a herd that size alone."

She started to climb into the truck but it was a high step up so she accepted the help he offered. His hand was big and strong, with long, lean fingers, and his palm was not nearly as tough as she'd expected.

Once she was seated and buckling up, he closed the door and came around to slide behind the wheel. Just as he was going to start the engine, his cell phone buzzed and he took a quick look at it. Then he checked his watch.

"Honestly, you don't have to drive me anywhere," Hannah said. "I can wait for Rachel or Nikki."

"If it was a problem, I'd tell you. I don't have anything I need to do at the moment." He put his phone on the console and started the truck. A country music song blasted from the speakers and he quickly turned off the radio. "I wanted to get away from the ranch for a while. That's all."

"You were in the bar for less than an hour. That's not much of a—" She sighed at the smile tugging at his mouth. Okay, so she'd noticed him when he'd first come in. So what?

At the sound of laughter she turned and saw two couples leaving a steak house. Once they were on the sidewalk, the women tried awfully hard to see through the truck's tinted windows. The shorter brunette smiled and waved.

Seth waved back. "So," he said, "what do you want

to do? Go straight to the Sundance? Go for a ride? Get something to eat?"

Excitement flared, then the truth hit her. "That tricky little—Rachel had me convinced this was all because she had to run to get a part for Matt. I swear I'm gonna kill her."

"I don't think I can help you with that," he said, and pulled the truck away from the curb. "But I will need to know which direction to go."

"The Sundance, I guess," Hannah said, and he looked disappointed, so that was some consolation. "How well do you know her?"

"Rachel? Not all that well. We went to different high schools. I know her brothers."

"Well, I love her dearly but she has a nasty little habit of trying to fix up her friends. Or anyone." Hannah snorted. "She's horrible about it."

"Oh, that's right," he said with a slow nod. "She used to piss off Cole and Jesse."

"Yeah, that doesn't surprise me one bit." Hannah cleared her throat. "Anyway, I'm pretty sure that's why she asked you to give me a ride. I mean, I'm only here for a week, but—well, who knows what she was thinking…"

Seth didn't respond. He had no reaction at all, and not because he needed to pay attention to traffic. Main Street was practically dead.

"Another thing you should know—I didn't say anything to her about you. So if she is trying to hook us up, it's all her doing." She stared at his thin, high-bridged nose, waiting, knowing he'd heard her. But he kept his eyes on the road.

Maybe she shouldn't have brought it up. He'd drop her off at the Sundance and she'd never see him again. The idea was surprisingly disappointing. She was still staring at him when he finally turned to look at her. Hannah pretended she was looking past him at the well-lit service station, the last vestige of civilization before the highway stretched into darkness.

"Are you waiting for me to say I have a problem with that?" he asked. "Because I don't."

"Which part?"

"Any of it."

Hannah wasn't sure what to make of that. Obviously he didn't care about Rachel's meddling. But did he also mean he was open to hooking up? "Well, neither do I," she said, her heart pounding as she watched a slow, telling smile curve his mouth.

After driving for another mile or better, she still couldn't think of anything more to say. And clearly he didn't feel the need to contribute. Normally she was fine with silence, but not knowing where they stood was maddening.

As it was, she couldn't stop herself from glancing over at him every few seconds. His hand was on the steering wheel, and his T-shirt exposed his muscled arm. The short sleeve clung to his well-defined biceps.

"Why aren't you staying with Rachel and Matt?"

"I had a conflict and couldn't make it to their wedding, so I just met Matt today. Seems like a great guy. And of course he would be…" Hannah shrugged. "I don't know. I guess I didn't want to get in the way. A week's a long time to have a houseguest."

"I see your point. Summer is a busy season, though I don't think Rachel is involved in the day-to-day operation."

"No, but she's at the Sundance every day. The dude ranch keeps her hopping even though she and Jamie split duties." She saw his brows lower in a frown. "Cole's wife, the woman who was with us at the Watering Hole. She's handling reservations, meals, that sort of thing, and Rachel takes guests on trail rides and gives riding lessons so she doesn't have to pull any of the men away from the cattle side."

"That doesn't sound like much fun for you. Unless you're going to help with the lessons."

Hannah cursed her big mouth. It would've been so much easier if he didn't know about her parents' ranch. "I don't ride well enough."

Seth glanced over at her. "You grew up on a ranch."

"I'm aware," she said with a forced laugh.

"Did you use ATVs?"

It was tempting to lie and say yes, but she wasn't good with those either. "My dad didn't like me hanging around while he was working, so I just…" She shrugged. "Read a lot of books. Where's your ranch in relation to the Sundance?"

He didn't seem eager to answer. For God's sake, it was an idle question. Only meant to change the subject. It wasn't as if she planned on showing up uninvited.

"About thirty minutes, give or take," he said with a faint smile. "Depending on traffic."

Hannah grinned. "I saw a truck hauling a horse trailer. I can see how the streets might get congested."

Seth briefly took his eyes off the road to look at her. "Assuming Rachel's going to be busy, what are you doing tomorrow?"

"Um, nothing, really. I'm going to try to sleep in, a long shot at best." She wound her fingers together, a nervous habit she thought she'd broken years ago. This wasn't like her, being hesitant. "You have something in mind?"

"Oh, quite a few things," he said, his laugh as deep

and gravelly as his voice. "Are you interested in seeing the sights? Not that there's much around here but you might enjoy a drive to Glacier National Park. After that we could get some dinner."

"Not much here? The Rockies are practically in your backyard." She turned to look out the window. Even in the gathering darkness, she could see the distant snow-topped peaks jutting into the night sky. And, of course, the stars. Hundreds and hundreds, maybe even thousands. She sighed and turned back to Seth. "Yes. I'd love to, thank you."

"Good. You sleep in and I'll get the men squared away for the day, then we'll make it happen," he said. "What was the sigh for?"

"I still can't get over the stars. I don't remember the sky ever looking this spectacular at home."

"Are you in a hurry to get to the Sundance?"

"Not at all," she said, stifling a yawn. Travel days were always hard, but she wasn't about to miss out on anything Seth had to offer.

"Then how about we take a short detour?"

"I'm game if you are."

"In about a mile we're going to leave the highway. It'll be bumpy for a while as the road climbs into the foothills, but it's not too steep. Still game?"

She kind of wanted him to define *not too steep*. But come on, did it really matter? "Of course."

"So, what is it you do in Dallas?" he asked, as soon as he'd made the turn.

"Executive recruiter," she said, grabbing on to the handhold over the door. "I match qualified candidates with the right jobs. It can be interesting. The fun part is getting to learn about how different businesses work."

"Do you recruit on behalf of corporations or individuals?"

"Mostly corporations. Though I also have a list of execs who aren't looking for jobs actively, but if one comes along that I think would be of interest, I let them know."

"Sounds challenging." Seth slowed down as they arrived at a small clearing, the headlights sweeping clusters of purple and yellow wildflowers.

He got out of the truck, and while he rummaged around in the back, she popped a breath mint.

"You want some water?" he asked.

"Maybe later," she said, as she slid off the seat. "Isn't it late for wildflowers?"

"It's the altitude. They're on their way out. Last month you would've seen five times as many. I'm getting a blanket. Pick a spot."

A shiver raced down her spine. Impressive as the wildflowers were, all she could think was…blanket! She had a good feeling there'd be more making out than stargazing going on. And, boy, was she ready.

She looked up at the sky. None of the surrounding trees blocked their view of the moon and stars. The clearing was perfect. And, for now, so was the cowboy walking toward her.

Hannah's goals had been to visit Rachel and get the hell away from Texas and her father—the man made her so crazy she could forget how to breathe. Vacay sex hadn't consciously been on the list. But this was a nice bonus. Not only had Rachel vouched for Seth, but Hannah lucking out the first day? Amazing.

"Is this the spot you want?"

"Oh, sorry, I've been looking up instead of down."

All he did was smile at her and her heart beat wildly.

Thankfully, he'd brought two bottles of water with him. Her mouth was suddenly dry and she sucked greedily on the mint. Probably looked obscene. She turned away and toed the hard ground. Most of the clearing was covered by tall grass.

"I think the best we can hope for is no rocks." Seth nodded to an area where the grass had been flattened. "Deer approved. Shall we try it?"

He checked for rocks while taking quick glances up at the sky. Hannah did the same thing on the other side. An aspen that had provided the deer with shade blocked a tiny section of stars but the rest of the trees were slender pines.

"This is fine with me," she said, and helped him spread the blanket out on the ground. "What? No pillows?"

Seth chuckled. "You've lived in Dallas too long."

"And yet, not long enough," she muttered, and saw his curious look. "Family stuff. Moving three states away from my dad would've been better."

"I get it," Seth said with a wry smile. "I joined the air force."

"Wow. For how long?"

"Four years." Crouching, he folded back part of the blanket, avoiding her gaze, and she wondered if he regretted telling her.

"Should I be doing the same thing on this side?"

"No, it's fine," he said, and flattened more of the grass before smoothing the blanket over it. "Here's your pillow, princess."

Hannah laughed. "I was joking," she said, then pinned him with a mock glare. "Princess? Ha. Far from it."

"Come here."

"Don't you mean, come here, please?" She watched a shadow cross his face and realized a cloud had passed over the moon. It made him look a little dangerous, certainly mysterious and too damn sexy. He could've just snapped his fingers and she would've scurried over to him.

"Please," he said.

She gave a final tug on her side. It wasn't necessary but it bought her a few seconds to calm down. "Where do you want me?"

"Right here." He caught her arm and gently pulled her closer. Once she was directly in front of him, he turned her around and put a hand on her right shoulder. "Now, look up. How's this view?"

Hannah felt his heat against her back, felt the steady, gentle presence of his palm cupping her shoulder. "Perfect," she whispered.

His warm breath tickled the side of her neck. He pressed his lips against her skin. "You smell good," he murmured, running his hand down her arm to lightly grip her elbow. With his other hand he swept the hair away from her neck. His breath stirred the loose strands at the side of her face.

Hannah was too dizzy to think of one damn thing to say. She saw a pair of eerie, yellowish eyes in the trees, low to the ground, before they disappeared. A howl split the night. She stifled a shriek, whirled and threw her arms around Seth's neck.

He enfolded her in his strong, muscled arms and held her close. "It's nowhere near us."

"I don't know why it made me jumpy," she said, embarrassed but loving the feel of his hard body flush with hers. "I'm used to coyotes."

"That was a wolf."

Wolf? She didn't know anything about them. Did they run from humans or put them on the menu? She leaned back and looked up at him. Before she could question whether or not this was a good idea, Seth lowered his head.

Their lips touched and she was lost in the fog.

3

THE TEMPERATURE HAD dropped since the sun went down. But the chilly air wasn't the reason Hannah pressed herself against his warm body. Enticed by the pleasant muskiness of his skin, by his firm lips moving over hers, she tightened her hold around his neck.

Seth pulled her closer. The heat of his erection penetrated both layers of their denim jeans. The urge to move her hips was too great to ignore. She swayed a little to the left.

He froze, all of him, his body, his mouth, the hand that had started rubbing her back. A low groan rumbled deep in his throat. She felt it against her lips, followed by a jolt of excitement that traveled all the way down her spine.

It didn't take much for him to tease her lips apart. She readily opened for him and welcomed the thrust of his tongue. He tasted as good as he smelled—200 percent male. A rush of warmth spread through her body and settled into dampness between her thighs. She arched into him and he deepened the kiss.

Easing her death grip on his neck, she was able to run her fingers through his hair, touch his muscled chest. But the brief time-out was enough to make her wonder what the hell she was doing. She'd just met the man. Kissing was fine, for tonight. They still had tomorrow. Hopefully, she'd see a lot of him the whole week.

He must've sensed her hesitation. He broke the kiss and gave her a questioning look.

"We're still standing," she said in a playful tone.

"Yes, we are."

Despite her rude awakening, Hannah wasn't anxious to pull away. And, it seemed, neither was Seth.

Finally he stepped back and expansively spread his hand. "Your blanket and pillow await."

"Lucky for you, you left out *princess*."

He grinned. "Why? What would you have done?"

"It's more like what I wouldn't have done."

He gave it a moment's thought. "Ah," he said, with a solemn nod. "Yeah, lucky I didn't."

Hannah laughed as she lowered herself to the blanket. By plopping down in the center, she couldn't have made it more obvious that she wanted him to sit next to her.

After grabbing the water he'd left on the hood, he joined her, stretching out his long legs and passing her a bottle. He sat close enough that their shoulders brushed and tilted his head back to look up at the sky.

Hannah would've been content just to stare at him. But she followed his gaze to the crescent moon hovering over the Rockies. "How many constellations are there? Do you know?"

"Close to ninety have been recognized."

"Do you know all their names?"

Seth laughed. "That's a tall order."

The air really was too chilly for her short sleeve shirt, and she leaned closer to him. "You didn't answer my question."

"Maybe at my geekiest."

"Oh, please. You were never a geek."

He smiled at her, then frowned when he caught her shivering. Wrapping an arm around her shoulders, he pulled her against his side. "I might have a long-sleeved shirt in the truck," he said, brushing the hair away from her face. "Or we don't have to sit out here at all."

"No, I like it here," she said quickly. "Unless it's too cool for you."

"Not with you snuggled up to me like this, it isn't."

"Feels perfect to me." Weird, very weird, in fact, and yet perfect.

Sitting like this was something she associated with boyfriends. Cuddling and holding hands felt intimate to her, and often uncomfortable. Of course she'd gone out with a few guys she liked over the years. Shane was strictly a friend. Trevor and Steve were more like sex buddies with no expectations on either side. True intimacy had never played a part in any of her relationships. Yet sitting here with Seth felt perfectly normal. Safe, even. Pleasant. And how did that make sense?

"I think I'll go look for that shirt," he said, removing his arm from her shoulders.

"Look, if you're cold we'll go. No problem."

"Not for me. You're the one shivering."

"Was I?" She heard another howl and jumped. "Still far away, right?"

"Right," he said, and started to get to his feet, but she caught his arm.

"I'm not cold."

"Okay. But let's try this instead." He resettled on the blanket, this time behind her. "How about you sit here," he said, patting the spot between his spread legs.

Her pulse fluttered. "That doesn't look comfortable for you."

"Sure it is." He drew up his bent knees so she could shift into place.

She refused to check if his erection had subsided. Surely it must have or he wouldn't have made the offer. Still, she hesitated to lean back, until his coaxing won her over. Her shoulders met his chest, but she managed to leave some room behind her butt to avoid contact.

"Better?" he asked, wrapping his arms around her. "You're stiff. Relax. I'm not going to bite."

"Any chance you have a can of wolf repellent in your truck?"

Seth chuckled. "Is that what's got you tense?" His mouth was near her right ear; his warm breath glided over her skin at the side of her neck. "The wolves aren't going to bother us," he murmured.

Oh, God, his body was so warm, chasing away the chill air. His encircling arms were strong and made her feel ridiculously safe. So safe she found her butt snuggled up against his…his crotch. Anatomically, no other body part was possible. And his arms made it all the way around her drawn-up knees. Yet his hold remained loose. She didn't feel the urge to break free just to make sure she could.

He'd told her to relax. She was practically lounging back as if he was the most comfy chair in the world. His heart was beating a bit fast, and so was hers.

"You okay?" he asked.

"I'd feel a whole lot better if I thought you were more comfortable."

"Are you kidding? What could be better than this?"

"Um…" Hannah laughed. "Nothing."

"Besides that," he said, and kissed her neck.

She felt a jerky movement against her backside and she bit down on her lip. "Ouch!"

He brought his head up. "Did I hurt you?"

"It was me. I bit my lip."

"Let's see."

"It's okay. I'll live."

He cupped her chin and turned her face toward him. "You have pretty lips."

"What?" Hannah giggled.

"Soft, too," he said, drawing his thumb over them. He bent his head as if he were about to kiss her, but it wasn't easy, the way they were sitting.

Their mouths merely brushed.

Hannah sighed, completely ready to give up warmth for more kissing. But Seth didn't seem to be of the same mind. He just smiled and settled back.

"Hey, look at that," she said, pointing to the western sky. "Are those stars in the shape of a W, or is it my imagination?"

"That's Cassiopeia," he said, without enthusiasm.

"Not your favorite, huh?"

"I wouldn't kick her out of bed," he said, and grinned when Hannah twisted around to give him a look. "We see Cassiopeia all year long from here. Now, if it was October or November, the bottom of the W would point to Andromeda."

"What about that one?"

His cheek close to hers, he followed her gaze. "That's Cygnus. We can only see it during the summer."

"It looks like a kite."

"According to mythology it's supposed to be the form of a swan that Zeus used to seduce women."

"Okay, you need quite an imagination to come up with that description," Hannah muttered, trying to not get too distracted by the feel of Seth's cheek pressed against hers. "What about the W? What's the story behind that one?"

"Queen Cassiopeia sitting on her throne combing her hair. Her claim that she was more beautiful than the gods pissed off Poseidon, so he put her in the sky as punishment."

Hannah grinned. "Those touchy Greeks." She moved, just to see him better. "I doubt you were trying to impress me, but wow anyway."

He smiled and went for a kiss. Their lips almost met, but not quite. The slightly different position wasn't any better.

"Okay, this isn't working," he said. "You mind scooting down a couple feet?"

She didn't need to think about it. She just slid her butt to the edge of the blanket. Seth pulled the opposite end up, draping it over her shoulders as he settled beside her.

"How's that?" he asked, keeping his arm around her.

"Perfect." She smiled at him and he pressed his lips to her mouth.

The sudden kiss startled her at first, but then she kissed him back. His arm tightened around her shoulders as his tongue swept past her lips and probed her mouth. He wasn't in a hurry, but that didn't make the kiss less intense. With his free hand he cupped her jaw as they explored each other, her breasts aching for his touch.

She lifted a hand to his chest and felt the swell of muscle under her palm. His heart pounded as hard and fast as her own. Shifting to give herself more freedom of movement, she nearly forced him back flat onto the blanket.

The kiss broke. Laughing and out of breath, she barely had the strength to help hold him upright. Not that she was doing anything more than clutching his shoulder.

"What are you doing?" Seth asked, also laughing.

"I'm not sure."

He used an elbow to brace himself and she landed, half

sprawled across his body, her breasts squashed against his chest.

She wasn't too upset with the awkward move, though. Their new position had its upside. "Did I bruise you for life?"

"They should fade in a week or so."

"Sorry. I was actually trying to prevent this from happening," she said, and realized that righting herself would go a long way toward reinforcing that claim. Grudgingly she started lifting herself off him.

Seth stopped her. "The ground isn't too bad if you want to try lying back."

"Or you make a pretty decent body pillow."

"Sure, feel free to use me."

Grinning, Hannah moved her arm and unintentionally brushed his erection.

He hissed through gritted teeth. "Yeah, sitting is probably better."

"I didn't do that on purpose," Hannah said, her breathy voice sounding strange to her ears.

"I know."

She didn't even try to hide her disappointment when he sat upright. Instead she almost gave in to the urge to cup him, make sure he knew it was no accident. But that wouldn't be cool. She'd never had sex with a guy the same day she met him and she'd already decided making out would be enough for tonight.

The stars seemed to be multiplying, each one trying to outshine the others. Barely covering a yawn in time, she felt his hand close gently on the nape of her neck.

"Tired?" he asked.

"A little."

"I should've taken you straight to the Sundance."

Hannah gaped at him. "No way. And miss this?"

"Don't worry. In a week you'll see your fill of stars."

"That's not what I meant," she said, and felt the pressure at her nape become a gentle massage.

They leaned into a soft kiss. Hannah laughed when they both angled their heads the same way.

Seth didn't. He cupped her face with one hand and deepened the kiss, their tongues touching and stroking each other. His hand moved to her neckline, and he toyed with the fabric before dipping his fingers just underneath, just enough to tease.

She trembled when his mouth left hers and his lips blazed a damp path down the side of her neck.

Gently, he touched her jaw, then trailed his fingertips down her throat over her knit top and lingered between her breasts. The inside of his wrist grazed her hardened nipple.

Hannah held her breath. The tiny movement caused a slight thrust of her breasts. She waited, wondering if he'd slip his hand under her shirt.

The temptation was there. She could feel his tension, his indecision, his restraint. Damn, she wished she could see his face. But it was impossible with the way they were sitting. Although she could see his straining fly just fine.

She laid a hand on his thigh, about midway between his knee and groin. And then she inched higher, stopping short of his erection. His free hand went to the back of her head and he held her still while he kissed her.

Oh, God, she wanted to touch him so badly. But she didn't dare. His mouth was hot and hungry, his skin feverish, his warm rugged scent surrounded her. It was all going to her head. Stepping just one toe over the line would be all it took. They wouldn't stop. And there would be no do-overs. She wasn't sure it mattered.

Seth was waiting for her to make the next move, she

realized. She'd set the tone and he could've taken over from there, but he wanted her to call that final shot. While she appreciated his thoughtfulness, she almost wished he'd just gone for it.

A cool breeze seemed to come out of nowhere, nipping at her, making her shiver. She rubbed her bare arms. Removing her hand from his thigh killed the mood.

He straightened away from her. "Guess I'm doing a shitty job."

"Oh, no." Hannah clutched at his arm, trying to bring him back to her. "It feels good."

"I meant keeping you warm."

"Ah. Right." She gave him a sheepish smile. "No, it was just that one little gust."

"Gust?" Seth laughed. "I'd stay away from Montana in the winter if I were you." He grabbed both their waters. "In the meantime, let's get out of here."

"We don't have to go." A yawn threatened and she pressed her lips together for a second. "It was just that one…breeze."

"Look, you have a whole week. No rush, right?"

She would've rather he'd said *we*. But that might've sounded too presumptuous. Probably not something she would've said herself. "I've ruined the night, haven't I?"

"Absolutely not," he said as he got to his feet. "I've enjoyed myself."

She grasped his outstretched hand and he pulled her up.

"Go ahead and get in the truck," he said when she picked up one side of the blanket.

"I'm really not cold."

"Just tired."

Hannah sighed. "Exhausted," she admitted. "It was harder getting away from the office than I thought."

"Signs of a healthy economy, right?"

"More like a slave-driver boss."

Seth smiled, and boy did she want to kick herself. It was only a little after ten. She was on vacation and had lucked out meeting a gorgeous guy the very first night. And what was she doing? Squandering an opportunity to get laid, that's what.

"Hannah?"

She blinked at Seth as he tried to take her corner of the blanket from her.

With a wicked smile that made her wonder if she'd said something she shouldn't have, he tugged the blanket free of her hand. "Come on," he said. "Let's get you to bed."

4

HANNAH STARTED DOWN the staircase, but was so busy rereading a text from Seth confirming their date that she nearly missed a step. She grabbed the oak handrail and managed to hang on to the mug of coffee she'd gotten from the kitchen earlier.

It was her third one. She was more than half awake. Hopefully this would finish the job. The last thing she wanted was to be yawning all day. And all because some idiot had raised his voice outside her window at 6:00 a.m.

She didn't know who it was, or who he'd been yelling at. All she really knew was that it had something to do with the upcoming town meeting and grazing permits. She'd have to ask Rachel about it later. Without letting on about the rude wakeup call. Anyway, it was Hannah's own fault for being too snug under the covers and not closing her window.

Chatter drifted from the dining room, but she stopped for a moment to look out at the Rocky Mountains through the expansive two-story windows. Lucky her, she was staying on the same floor as the family, and not in the separate wing where they put regular Sundance guests.

She envied Rachel, growing up in this house, with

this view every day. Today the sky was clear and a perfect blue; not even the slightest trace of smog blurred the edges. Hannah had been living in Dallas an awfully long time, and on the rare weekends she went home to see her parents, she always ended up too stressed to truly appreciate the beautiful country mornings.

It was hard to believe the McAllisters' original house had started off as a modest-sized log cabin over a hundred years ago. It probably hadn't been all that much bigger than the current foyer that spilled into the dining room on one side and the living room on the other.

Sitting at the table with Rachel's mom were three other guests. Carol, whom Hannah had met last night, smiled. The other two women sent her bored looks before returning to their muffins.

"Good morning, Hannah," Barbara McAllister said with a bright smile. "Rachel's looking for you. She's taking a group on a trail ride this morning and wanted to know if you'd like to join them."

"Ah, sounds like fun," she said, lying through her teeth. She hadn't been on a horse in fifteen years. "But I can't. I have a date."

All three women turned their heads to give her a second look.

"Didn't you just arrive yesterday?" The blonde stared with a hint of accusation in her narrowed eyes.

"Yes, I'm Hannah," she said, crossing to the table with her hand extended. She should've left out the date part. Rachel had warned her many of the guests came here looking for vacay sex.

"Kimberly," the woman muttered, accepting the gesture with a limp handshake.

The third woman made no effort to introduce herself so Hannah let it go.

"You work fast," Carol said with a laugh. "We were just telling Mrs. McAllister she should've had more good-looking sons."

"Available ones," Kimberly added. "We came too late. They've all been snatched up."

Shaking her head, Barbara laughed. Trim, petite and with the same lively green eyes as her daughter, she looked more like she was pushing fifty instead of sixty.

"If it's any consolation, Rachel and I were in the same sorority together for three years and she never told me they were hot. Just that she had brothers." Hannah gave Barbara a private smile as she came around the table and took the chair beside her.

"That's just wrong." Carol's warm smile made up for the other two sourpusses. "And you're still friends."

"Yep. Not sure why." Hannah nodded to the coffee Barbara offered. "Thank you."

"Have you eaten yet?" Barbara asked. "We have more muffins and fruit in the kitchen, and Hilda is making omelets."

"I had a muffin earlier, but thanks—"

"To be honest…" Kimberly cut her off. "I think Rachel should take their pictures off the website. It's almost—I don't know, false advertising or something."

"Oh, for goodness' sakes, this isn't a dating service." Barbara gave Kimberly the mom glare, that said, *open your mouth again and I'll wash it out with soap.* It was clear where Rachel got her backbone. "Anyway, if you are looking to…what is it?" She paused, waving a hand. "Hook up," Barbara said finally, and Hannah nearly spit out her coffee. "With so many hired men in the area, they outnumber the women three to one."

Kimberly blushed and sulked at the same time.

Carol burst out laughing.

The mystery brunette stared at Hannah. "Is it the guy who was sitting at the bar last night?" she asked. "At the Watering Hole?"

Hannah hesitated, tempted to ignore her. "Oh, were you there? Didn't see you. But to answer your question, yes."

"Well, wasn't that nice of Rachel to fix up her old friend," the woman said in a snippy tone.

Several juicy remarks sat primed on the tip of Hannah's tongue, but she restrained herself. Both women were very pretty and wouldn't need any help hooking up for the week. As long as they kept their rude mouths shut.

The front door opened and Hannah recognized Rachel's laugh. "Hey, look who I found," she said, drawing everyone's attention as she passed through the foyer.

Seth walked in behind her. He yanked off his black Stetson.

"Mornin', Mrs. McAllister. Ladies," he added with a brief nod at the other three women, and then he looked at Hannah. "Hello, Hannah." He gave her a slow, bone-melting smile. "Sorry I'm a little early. I figured I'd talk to Jesse for a while…"

"But I dragged him in here," Rachel said, her devilish grin directed at Hannah. "So, I guess that's a big no on the trail ride, huh?"

Determined to play it cool, Hannah rolled her eyes. Not easy with her heart trying to pound its way out of her chest. He wasn't wearing anything special. Just the typical cowboy get-up, boots, jeans, a blue button-down shirt. But he'd rolled the sleeves up to his elbows, exposing tanned muscular forearms, and for some reason that made her mouth go dry.

"Seth, it's so nice to see you." Barbara had shot to

her feet and was skirting the table. "It's been a while, hasn't it?"

"Yes, ma'am, it has," he said, bending as she pulled him into a fierce hug. He looked so tall next to her. And his shoulders were much broader than Hannah remembered from last night.

"How's the family—"

"The omelets are almost ready." Hilda said, as she pushed through the swinging door from the kitchen. Her dark eyes lit up when she saw him. "Oh, Seth, look at you...so tall and handsome."

Barbara stepped aside as Hilda rushed toward him.

"Hi, Mrs. Carter." He smiled and moved his Stetson out of harm's way in the nick of time.

The wiry housekeeper threw her arms around him. "I saw your mom at the market. She said you're here for good, this time."

"That's right. Dad's retired so I'm helping Clint run the Whispering Pines."

Hilda stood back, still holding on to one of his large hands. "Your mother is so happy. Did you know my Ben is back, too? He bought a ranch."

Seth nodded. "I ran into him at the hardware store a couple months ago."

Kimberly noisily cleared her throat. Once she had everyone's attention, she looked at Hilda. "Are our omelets getting cold?"

Throwing her hands up, Hilda muttered something in Spanish as she hurried toward the kitchen with Rachel on her heels.

"Come sit, Seth," Barbara said. "Have breakfast with us."

He darted a look at the other three women. Carol's smile was friendly. Kimberly and the brunette had their fangs out. Hannah would be taking several giant steps back if she were him.

"Have you eaten?" he asked her.

"Yes, but if you want—"

He shook his head. "I'd rather get on the road while it's not so hot. If that's okay with you."

"Sure." Hannah pushed her chair back, aware of the evil looks aimed at her.

"Thanks for the offer," he said to Barbara.

"Anytime, Seth. You're always welcome here. I hope you know that." She patted his arm. "Where are you two headed?"

Seth swept a gaze over Hannah as she left the table. He kept it brief but managed to linger a second too long on her bare legs. Long enough to make her a little flustered. "Glacier National Park," he said.

"Oh, you'll love it, Hannah. There's so much to see, you could spend a week watching the wildlife," Barbara said, just as Hilda came from the kitchen carrying plates of fluffy golden omelets.

Rachel held back the swinging door, and Barbara rushed over to help serve.

Hannah stopped. She'd almost forgotten. "I need to run upstairs and get my purse." She glanced down at her white shorts, pink tank top and strappy white sandals. "Am I dressed okay for the trip?"

"You look good to me," he murmured, his gaze missing nothing all the way down to her polished blue toenails.

Hannah didn't think it was her imagination that his voice had lowered. Or that his eyes had darkened. She hurried toward the stairs, aware he could watch her from where he was standing. She was also aware that Kimberly and her pal were breathing fire by now. Mostly he'd ignored them, though not in a discourteous way. But she had the feeling they weren't used to being outclassed by a woman who was barely a six.

"Hannah, wait."

On the second step she turned. One bad thing about an open floor plan, you couldn't get away with much. They weren't visible to everyone in the dining room but it was possible they could be overheard.

Seth came all the way to the stairs. "You should bring along some walking shoes," he said, then leaned so close that his breath tickled her ear. "It's going to be a long day. Wouldn't hurt to bring a change of clothes and some toiletries. I'll leave that up to you."

He straightened away from her and gave her another one of those irresistible smiles. Might as well hog-tie her and throw her in his truck. Like she could say no to anything that came out of his mouth.

"I have a question," she said.

"What's that?"

Standing on the second step gave her a two-inch advantage over him and this time she did the leaning, and whispered, "Why didn't I get a hug?"

"I was saving up for this." His hand cupped the back of her neck and he kissed her, the tip of his tongue taking a languid swipe with the promise of more to come.

Her toes curled over her sandals and she clutched his shoulders for balance. "I figured it was something like that," she said, pulling back and grinning. "Give me a few minutes to pack."

The self-satisfied gleam in his eyes caused a burst of excitement in her chest. Mingled laughter coming from the dining room abruptly changed the mood.

"Take your time," he said, settling his hat back on his head. "I'll be outside."

"Chicken," she whispered.

Seth just smiled and stayed right where he was...where she knew damn well he could watch her jiggling behind all the way up the stairs.

ALMOST THREE HOURS LATER, they entered the park. They'd made a stop that took them twenty minutes out of their way when Hannah realized she'd forgotten sunscreen. Seth wished they could've gotten an earlier start but he was lucky to get the whole day off, plus it was possible they'd spend the night, too. That would make up for a hell of a lot. Damn, he hoped it worked out. Since their time was limited, he'd decided Going-to-the-Sun Road was the best thing for them to do. The scenery was spectacular and it would give her a taste of everything from glacier-carved lakes and valleys to stunning jagged peaks. And wildlife. She seemed interested in spotting different critters and there would be lots of them.

"I can't believe all the snow," Hannah said, twisting around in her seat and staring out the back window at the snow-topped mountains all around them. "It's crazy."

"Considering it's only June there really isn't all that much. We're lucky Logan Pass isn't blocked. That's where we'll cross the Continental Divide."

She made the strangest noise. Kind of a strangled giggle. "I'm sure it won't be nearly as exciting as it sounds."

Seth chuckled. "Maybe it will, who knows?"

"How many times have you been here?"

"Over a hundred."

She swung her attention to him. "Are you serious?"

"Yep. I used to camp out here with my brothers when we were teenagers. Usually at the end of July or in August, when it's warmer. Less likely for the higher elevations to be blocked by snow."

"Oh, my God."

He slid her a quick glance.

Her gaze had wandered beyond him out the driver's window. "I think I just saw a bear."

"You might have." Unlikely at this elevation, but it was fun to see how excited she got over everything.

"He wasn't all that far from the road." Eyes narrowed, she craned her neck to see behind them.

"Do you want me to slow down?" Seth asked, even though they were practically crawling.

"For the bear?"

"No," he said, trying not to laugh.

"I knew that." She shifted so she was facing straight ahead. "I read there's a bunch of scenic turnouts. Would you mind stopping at a few?" It took all of three seconds for her to whip around again. "I'm never going to see everything."

"That's right, you won't. Not in one day." He should've warned her about first-timers overload. "So better you save yourself from whiplash and just concentrate on what's ahead."

"Am I annoying you?"

"Of course not." Trying to avoid the scurrying chipmunks, he kept his eyes on the road. But he found her hand and squeezed it. "It's fun being here with a virgin."

"Yeah, well, I hate to disappoint you…"

Seth laughed. Hannah was sharp, had guts and a great sense of humor, as she'd proven last night at the Watering Hole. And she had a slightly gullible streak that surfaced now and then. What he hadn't figured out—yet—was just how much of it was her yanking his chain. But either way, she made him smile, and few things had done that in the last couple of years.

"Hey, I should've told you before now. Cell service

is about to get real spotty. It's like that throughout most of the park, so if you need to call or text anyone, now's the time."

"Nope. I'm good."

Hell, he realized something else he should've considered and pulled the truck over the second he could.

Hannah dragged her gaze away from a pair of marmots lounging in the underbrush and looked at him. "Do you have to make a call?" she asked. "Because I definitely don't."

"We should talk about tonight." He checked the rearview mirror to make sure they were in the clear, then met her soft brown eyes and almost forgot why he'd stopped.

"I'm cool with staying overnight. I assume they have lodges or motels here?"

"They do," he said, lifting a hand to her cheek because he couldn't seem to stop himself. He stroked her smooth skin with his fingertips, touched the soft silky strands of her hair. He liked how the different shades of brown shimmered in the sunlight. "I don't know about availability so we'll have to call around."

Her lids drooped as she pressed her cheek against his palm. "Do you think we'll have trouble?"

"Not in June. It's just that the accommodations in the park can be a little rough."

Her sleepy eyes widened. "We have to camp?"

"Not that bad."

"I don't actually mind camping. I just prefer a heads-up."

He watched her chest rise with the deep breath she took. The tank top she was wearing wasn't too snug but fit close enough that it distracted him if he wasn't careful. Damn, he wanted to kiss her.

His cell rang, startling both of them.

It took some effort to dig for it in his jeans pocket. Especially with a partial erection in the way. Which he figured Hannah had also noticed because she turned abruptly to look out her window.

He saw that it was Paxton, one of the men from the Whispering Pines. That usually meant trouble. "Yeah, Paxton…"

"Hey, boss. You busy?"

Seth knew that sheepish tone all too well. And calling him boss? "What do you want?"

"You happen to be anywhere nearby?"

"Why?"

"I kinda lost the key to the medicine cabinet."

"Kinda?" Seth glanced at the dashboard clock. Already noon. Paxton should've given the pregnant mares their meds by now. "Either you lost it or you didn't."

Paxton noisily cleared his throat. "I had it earlier. Then I misplaced the damn thing. It's gotta turn up. You got one, don't you?"

"Where's Clint?"

"He and Lila left for Kalispell about an hour ago. Won't be back till late."

Seth pinched the bridge of his nose. Kalispell was closer to the Whispering Pines, but he wouldn't ask Clint to drive back. The poor guy deserved the time off with Lila. Hell, what he truly deserved was to be able to count on Seth for a change.

He looked over at Hannah. She'd been gazing out the window but she turned to him with a smile. She could only glean so much from his side of the conversation but she mouthed, "It's fine."

Cursing to himself, Seth exhaled slowly. She'd never know how much he appreciated her understanding. Though he doubted she understood their entire day and night together was about to be ruined. Maybe the whole week. He didn't know if he could take another day off. But, hell, he owed his brother. His whole family.

After a nervous silence, Paxton asked, "You want me to give Clint a holler?"

"No. It'll take me about three hours," he said, and couldn't quite look at Hannah.

"Sorry, boss," Paxton mumbled.

"Yeah. I know." Seth disconnected the call and put the phone down with too much force. "Son of a bitch." He turned to Hannah. "I'm sorry."

"Oh, please. I can curse with the best of 'em."

He managed a smile. "About everything. I have to get back to the Whispering Pines."

"I guessed as much."

"After that, it'll be too late to come back here." He saw the disappointment in her eyes. Just a flicker and then it was gone. She wouldn't sulk or make him feel bad, like so many other women he knew. The thing was, they could still drive to Kalispell afterward, just to have dinner and spend the night. For that matter, there was a motel in Blackfoot Falls. But either option seemed too tacky. He wouldn't feel right doing that to her.

"Shouldn't we be getting back on the road?" she asked softly. "I'm not trying to rush you. It just sounded kind of important."

"Hannah…"

"I know, Seth. It's fine. I promise. Not having a nine-to-five job has its trade-offs."

"Tell me about it," he said, and started the truck. Throw in a few years of penance on top of that…yeah, he'd pretty much have no life for the next decade.

"I'm going to ask you something and I want you to swear you'll tell me the truth."

"You got it," he said. "Shoot."

"Would you mind if I went with you? Maybe I can even help."

Seth had shifted the truck into gear but paused to look into her earnest brown eyes. "I'll even give you the grand tour," he said, leaning over the inconvenient center console. He didn't care if he was parked at the side of the road. He was going to kiss this woman, and kiss her well.

5

WITH THE SUN beating through the window on Hannah's side of the truck for most of the return trip, thirty minutes from the Whispering Pines she began to feel drowsy.

They'd picked up sodas and snacks in Kalispell. She knew Seth had stopped for her benefit, even though she'd told him it wasn't necessary. Thank goodness he hadn't listened to her. She took another sip of her cola, hoping the caffeine would revive her. In the meantime, she laid her head back, her droopy eyelids hidden behind her sunglasses.

In a way it was good that Seth's parents were away visiting family in Missoula. His brother Clint and his fiancée, Lila, wouldn't be there, either. It wasn't that Hannah didn't want to meet them. She just preferred being at her sparkling best for an introduction.

"Something else I should warn you about," Seth said, and she brought her head up. "Murray does most of the cooking in the bunkhouse. If he offers you anything to eat, turn it down."

"Lousy cook?"

"Hard to tell. He puts so damn many hot peppers in

everything. Doesn't matter what he's cooking. Whatever it is, I can guarantee it'll blow your head off."

"Excuse me, mister, but I'm a Texan. There is nothing too spicy for me."

"Okay," he said, clearly amused. "We'll see about that. Hey, you know anything about weddings?"

"Weddings?" Hannah blinked. Weird segue. "What, I don't get a ring first?"

Seth choked out a laugh. "Clint and Lila are getting married next month. The reception is going to be at the ranch, and between our mom and Lila's, so far the guest list has topped five hundred."

"Holy crap!"

"Not unusual around here, though. Everyone thinks they should be invited."

"So, how do you accommodate that many people? A tent?"

"At this rate, probably two of 'em. I suggested fixing up the barn—"

Hannah started laughing and snorted soda up her nose.

"Hey, that's a better response than I got from my mom." Seth glanced over at her. "You okay?"

She nodded and wiped her face with a napkin. "Are you serious about the barn? Was that your question?"

"I didn't mean we'd leave it as is. We could clean it up and partition off anything unsightly. They're going to decorate anything that doesn't move, anyway."

"Well, it's kind of a trend in Texas." Although Hannah didn't see the appeal. "You must be reading bridal magazines."

"Yeah, right. It just makes sense. July is a hot month. The barn would be cooler."

"Ah." Hannah had to admit, he had a point. "What did your brother say?"

"He's staying out of it."

"Smart man."

"Guess that makes me the dumb ass."

"Your words, not mine." She caught the beginning of a smile before she turned her head to scope out the scenery. She loved the area. The green rolling hills on one side of the highway were dotted with grazing cattle, hundreds of them as far as she could see. To her right, scrub brush gave way to the foothills, covered with pines and aspens and other trees. In the background were the Rockies. A few hours ago, she and Seth had been right there, so close. "It's beautiful here. Whispering Pines is the perfect name."

Seth's smile lacked its usual warmth. "You're a good sport, Hannah. This is a hell of a way to spend a day of your vacation."

"Are you kidding? I'm so lucky. The girls back at the Sundance are all green with envy. Not that I'm one to gloat." She paused. "Though two of them kinda deserve it, so I'm not promising anything."

His laugh made everything better and reset the tone. "How big is the Whispering Pines?"

"Twenty-five hundred acres now that we just purchased more land," he said, and frowned at her phony cough. "What?"

"That's a lot of land."

"You sure you're from Texas?"

"Fair point. But not much of it looks like this," she said. "Will you tell me when we come up on your family's spread?"

"Most of the property stretches to the east and south, but we'll pass through some of our pastures before we get to the gate. Now, all this you see around us is BLM land."

She'd already pegged the foothills as government land

but not the hilly pastures. Up ahead, she saw even more cattle. "So, whoever owns this herd has a grazing permit, is that right?" When all she got was silence she turned to Seth and noticed his jaw had tightened. "I guess I'm not understanding how that works. And yet I get to lose sleep over it."

The look he shot her bordered on suspicion. "How so?"

"I left my window open last night and early this morning some idiot yelling something about grazing permits woke me. And I'm on the second floor."

Seth frowned. "Do you know who it was?"

"I didn't look. But he wasn't one of the McAllisters. He sounded older and his voice had a real twang to it."

Recognition flickered in Seth's face. He kept his eyes on the road but he'd piqued her curiosity...especially when he didn't volunteer any information.

"You know who it is, don't you?"

He hesitated. "I might."

"You can tell me. I promise not to hunt him down and do unspeakable things to his person."

He gave her a wry smile. "What difference would a name make? You don't know him."

"True." Jeez, she hoped Seth wasn't related to the guy. "Are we doing anything after you drop off the key? I mean, besides giving me a tour. No pressure, though. That's not why I asked to tag along."

"You have something in mind?" His voice dropped to a lower pitch, which she took to mean they were on the same page.

"Not really." She watched him, gauging his reaction, hoping she hadn't misread him. "Actually, I was kind of wondering if I packed for nothing."

Seth smiled. "Well, we can make sure that isn't the case."

"Good. Then I'll get that name out of you later."

He barked out a laugh. "You can try."

"You doubt me?" She looked at him over the top of her sunglasses. A faint smirk tugged at his mouth. "Oh, I see what you're doing. Very clever. It might even work."

"What am I doing? I'm driving."

"Uh-huh. I know your type. You're one of those stop-it-some-more kind of guys. Well, honey, you just wait. You'll be begging to spill every secret you know."

Shaking his head, his mouth twitching, he shifted in his seat.

She considered asking him if his jeans were too tight, but zipped her lips, instead. She could only pull off so much before she started laughing or blushing. Why was she so comfortable with him? Was it because after a few days of fun and games she'd be gone?

"You sound pretty damn confident."

"I do, don't I?"

"I guess if you can get up in front of a bar full of people and—"

"Okay, we're never going to speak of that again. Ever. You feel me?"

Seth abruptly pulled the truck over to the shoulder. Before she could get a word out he had his arms around her. "I do," he murmured against her mouth, and he kissed her, increasing the pressure on her lips until she opened for him.

She put a hand against his chest and felt the strong, steady beat of his heart. Hers wasn't nearly as controlled. It seemed to have filled her entire chest and was pounding its way out. He stroked his tongue into her mouth, slowly, thoroughly, until she wanted to rip his clothes off and climb all over him.

By the time he ended the kiss she had no air left in

her lungs. Seth didn't look completely together, either. Beneath her palm his heart was doing the tango. She lowered her hand and caught a fleeting glimpse of his erection. The poor guy was going to hurt himself if they didn't do something about that soon.

The thought alone made her shiver.

She leaned back. "*You feel me* must be the magic words."

Seth laughed. "Come on, Hannah. You're a bright woman." He put the truck in gear. "You can say 'roll over' and I'm all yours."

"Huh. Sounds promising."

"Buckle your seat belt."

She glanced down. "When did you unbuckle it?"

He just smiled and got them back on the road.

IT WAS THREE THIRTY by the time Seth turned onto the gravel road that led to the ranch. He debated calling Paxton to hoof it out to open the gate. Made of iron and pine posts, the sucker weighed a ton. Seth never really minded getting out to deal with it. But he was still pissed at Paxton. Losing a key wasn't minor. The guy was damn lucky he hadn't been off the property when he'd misplaced it.

"Is this your road or a public access?" Hannah asked, leaning forward to look out the windshield.

He tried like hell to keep his eyes off her breasts. But she wasn't making it easy. Between her straining against the seat belt and the thin, stretchy material of her top, he could almost see the outline of her nipple. He sure didn't need to get out of the truck with an erection. "It's ours, and so is the land on either side."

"Wow. The grass is so lush and pretty."

"For now."

"You keep saying that," she said. "Hey, I think I can make out some buildings to the right."

"That would be the stable and east barn. Beyond that is the bunkhouse and a couple of equipment sheds."

"Is the house on the left? I can maybe see it, too."

"Yep, that's the house." Sitting at the top of a rise, its alpine-style peaked roof was hard to miss.

"Oh, my God, look at that gate. It's so wide. I can't imagine how heavy it is."

"We haul lots of stock and equipment in and out of here."

Seth nixed the idea of calling Paxton. He decided it would do him some good to get out for a few minutes. Away from his perfect view of her jutting nipples. Although he'd have to climb back in at some point.

He pulled the truck to a stop and exhaled a harsh breath. For Christ's sake, he should just ask her to sit back. He looked over and saw her staring up at the old sign hanging over the gate. *Whispering Pines* had been carved into the wood by Elwin Landers, his great-grandfather.

"I'll only be a minute," he said, opening his door.

"Would you like me to drive through while you hold the gate?"

"Sure." He expected her to get out and walk around but she slid her butt over the console and plopped down behind the wheel.

She cupped a hand over the gearshift knob and frowned. "Now, what does this thing do?"

His mouth dropped open. Then he saw she was trying to hold back a smile and he laughed.

After she drove in and he closed the gate, he hopped into the passenger side. "Just keep going until the road splits and veer left."

"Got it." She had to lift her chin so she could see over the steering wheel.

"You can raise the seat, if you want."

"We're not going far. I'm okay."

Seth forced himself to keep his eyes above the spot where her hair touched her shoulders. Last night he would've described her as a brunette. In the sunlight, streaks of honey and gold changed the color. Watching the way her hair bounced, he wondered how it would feel brushing his bare chest.

"Are we headed toward those two guys?"

Seth snapped out of his daydream. Paxton and Murray were standing near the corrals watching them drive up.

"Yep, see if you can hit the one wearing the stupid Hawaiian shirt."

"Paxton?" she asked, grinning.

Murray took off his hat and waved them forward. Yeah, as if they couldn't see his bright orange T-shirt. The old guy was off the clock, but he rarely left the ranch anymore. Except to pick up supplies at the hardware store. Although Clint had just put a stop to that. By accident he'd found out Murray hadn't renewed his driver's license since he turned sixty-five.

The other two hired men, Heath and Joe, were off today, as well. But Seth saw Joe's truck parked in back of the bunkhouse where he lived with Paxton and Murray. Probably sleeping off a hangover. The kid liked to party, but his work never suffered for it.

Seth motioned to a place at the side of the barn for Hannah to park, then pulled a big ring of keys out of the glove box. Murray approached them as they climbed out.

"You let a girl drive your truck?" he asked, frowning at her and rubbing the top of his balding head.

Hannah just laughed.

"Don't mind him." Seth touched her back, setting her in the right direction. "He let his license expire three years ago so he's not allowed to drive any of the Whispering Pines vehicles."

"I ain't letting some government mucky-muck, who don't even know me, tell me whether or not I can drive."

"Hmm." Hannah nodded. "I never considered that, but you have a point there."

Murray narrowed his pale eyes. After a few seconds of studying her face, he broke out in a toothless grin. "I like you. You got a good head on your shoulders, young lady. Anyhow, I drive anything I want here on the property."

"Not my truck."

"Yes, Seth, we all know that," Murray grumbled, and stuck his hat back on his head.

Paxton walked around the corner, his gaze fixed on Hannah. "Hell, son, I didn't know I was interrupting something important," he told Seth. "You must be really pissed at me."

"That's putting it mildly." Seth didn't get a reaction, not that he expected one.

"Son?" Hannah repeated, her brows raised.

"It's just a thing we say sometimes," Seth said, shrugging. "Kind of ironic coming from Paxton, though, since he's twenty-six going on twelve."

Murray chuckled.

Seth passed him the ring of keys. "You mind making sure I get these back?"

"Sure thing."

Paxton continued to stare at Hannah. "You were at the Watering Hole last night..." he said, with a slow grin. "You did that song—"

"Nope." She cut him off. "Wasn't me," she said, putting out her hand. "Hi, I'm Hannah."

Seth hadn't realized Paxton was at the bar. Probably in

the back playing pool. But right now Seth was more interested in Hannah. How she shook each man's hand without giving a single hint she'd just lied to Paxton's face. And had done it successfully, given his puzzled frown.

Good thing to remember, Seth thought wryly. "I'm assuming you still haven't found the key."

Paxton sobered. "Not yet. But it has to turn up. I've only been in the stables, the barn and the bunkhouse."

"That's all?" Seth studied him, hoping like hell that Paxton hadn't been foolish enough to take the key with him into town after Seth had given it to him last night.

Paxton shoved a hand through his disheveled dark hair. "Yeah, I'm pretty sure."

"Okay. Keep looking for it. Anything else while I'm here?"

"Don't believe there is," Murray said. "You ain't had a day off for months. Go on and have a good time."

Feeling Hannah's eyes on him, Seth looked at her. "Come on. I'll show you around."

"Here? There ain't nothing to see."

Seth frowned at Murray. Something was up with him. He seemed a little nervous, which was unusual. Hardly anything ever bothered him.

"How can you say that?" Hannah swept a hand toward the foothills, then tilted her head back to look at the sky. "It's absolutely beautiful here."

Murray peered down the driveway, then looked at Seth. "You want me to saddle Orion for you?" he asked, sounding awfully eager. "The lady might like Clementine. That mare is as sweet as they come. Won't take me no time at all."

"Um, I think I'll pass." Hannah stepped back. "But it was nice meeting both of you."

"Same here," Paxton mumbled, squinting at her and scratching his head.

Seth wondered if she'd fess up to being the one who massacred that song. He checked his watch while hiding a smile.

Murray murmured something to Hannah, then asked, "You gonna be at the house, Seth?"

He looked up and studied the man for a few seconds before turning to Hannah. "Would you excuse me for just a minute?"

"Of course. Shall I wait in the truck?"

"You can stay right here. I'll be quick." Seth almost kissed her. The impulse caught him off guard.

She had a light sprinkling of freckles across her nose. He hadn't noticed them before, and with her dark hair and brown eyes, he hadn't expected to see any. He liked them.

They stood there smiling at each other until he heard Murray noisily clear his throat, then spit out his chew.

Jesus, Seth hated that stuff.

Paxton had already taken off for the barn, and Seth motioned with his chin for Murray to step aside with him.

"What's going on?"

Murray rubbed his gray-stubbled jaw. "Nothing."

Seth raised his brows. "How long have I known you?"

"I changed a few of your diapers, sonny boy. So don't go giving me that look."

"You seem awfully anxious to get rid of me. Must be for a reason."

"Well, I reckon you're about to find out," Murray said, shaking his head. "Don't say I didn't try."

Even before Seth turned around, the truck's rough engine and loud muffler told him who was rattling down the driveway.

Jasper Parsons.

The last person on earth Seth wanted to see.

Shit.

6

"HANNAH, I'M GOING to ask you to do me a favor."

"Sure," she said, surprised when Seth took her hand. "Anything."

"I know it won't be easy, but it would mean a lot to me." His gaze went to the noisy old green pickup leaving a trail of dust behind as it sped down the driveway toward them. "You're about to meet someone you may recognize. Please don't say anything. I'll explain later."

"Of course, but I really don't know anyone—"

Brakes squealing, the truck came to a stop just a few feet from them. The driver had cut it awfully close. Not to mention the dust from his tires floating up Hannah's nose. She wondered if wordlessly flipping him off meant her promise was still good.

She pulled her hand away from Seth and turned to cover up a sneeze.

"Christ almighty," Murray said, waving away the dust. "What the hell is wrong with you, Jasper? Bet you never got them brakes checked, neither."

Jasper, who'd just jumped out of the truck, was short and wiry, and moved with the vigor of a young man. But he looked to be close to Murray's age, only he had more hair and sported an old-fashioned mustache. Hannah would've remembered if she'd seen him before. Anyway, she and Murray might as well have been invisible.

Gravel crunched beneath Jasper's boots as he headed straight for Seth, whose mouth was pulled into a thin line. It didn't look as if he'd be throwing down a welcome mat. "You know better than to be going that fast down a driveway."

Jasper snorted a rusty laugh. "You're not the one who should be lecturing me on driving, Landers."

Hannah recognized the twang in his voice. She met Seth's eyes and clamped her lips together. He looked annoyed enough for both of them.

"You heard about that meeting on Tuesday," Jasper said. "They got signs posted all over town."

Seth didn't answer, just folded his arms across his chest.

"Sadie says a government man is coming to answer questions. Bullshit. They're just trying to scare us."

"The mayor's got no reason to lie," Murray said. "Sadie's a straight shooter."

"I'm not accusing her of anything. She just don't know better. She's a barkeep, not a rancher." Jasper swung his gaze to Hannah, as if he hadn't noticed her until now. No smile. No tug on his battered straw hat. She didn't exist to him. Fine with her.

Seth reached for her hand. "Come on, let's go."

"Hold on there." Jasper paused to spit on the ground, then glared at Seth. "I'm taking a head count. Got a lot of men showing up on Tuesday, even Bertram from the Broken Arrow outside of Kalispell will be at the meeting."

"What about the McAllister brothers?" Murray asked.

"Stubborn assholes, the whole lot of 'em. Gunderson's another one. That boy's as useless as tits on a boar pig.

Says he don't care what the government does with their land. His daddy must be rolling over in his grave. Wallace would've showed up at the meeting with a shotgun."

"Well, I'm with the McAllisters and Gunderson on this," Seth said and lightly squeezed Hannah's hand. "So, count me out."

Jasper's dark eyes blazed. "The hell you say." He moved to block Seth's path. "You gotta speak for the rest of us, boy. You know how to speak their lingo."

"What did I just tell you? It's not my fight."

"Yep, I heard you. Quite clearly, actually," Hannah said, and Seth gave her a faint smile. She wasn't being smart-alecky or looking for payback. The growing tension that had Seth clenching his jaw worried her.

Jasper ignored her. "You mean to say there are no Landers cattle grazing on BLM land?"

"If there are, they're strays."

"And what about Lucky 7 cattle?"

"We have nothing to do with my brother's ranch. You'll have to ask Nathan. But he'll give you the same answer."

Jasper continued to glare. "It don't matter where you stand on the issue. You know how to talk to those government people. Show 'em they can't pull the wool over our eyes with all their fancy legal talk."

"If that's what you're worried about, then hire an attorney." Seth stepped around the smaller man, tugging Hannah along with him.

"Don't you walk away. You owe me, boy."

"I don't owe you a damn thing, Parsons. My debt to you was paid in full." Seth kept walking, didn't even glance back.

"The judge let you off too easy."

A vein popped out at the side of Seth's neck, but he didn't turn around.

"I reckon you don't care about dragging your family's good name through all the muck again," Jasper called out. "Won't be easy on your dad with him being sick and all."

Seth cursed under his breath. His steps slowed. Anger radiated from him.

"Jesus H. Christ, Jasper," Murray said with a grunt of disgust. "Don't you know when to shut your pie hole?"

Hannah squeezed Seth's hand but she doubted he was aware of her standing beside him as he turned to face the horrible man. She held her breath, hoping the confrontation didn't get physical, while part of her wanted to slap Jasper upside the head herself.

"I suggest you tread lightly, Parsons," he said in an unexpectedly calm voice. "And get the hell off our property."

Instead of slinking away like he should've done, Jasper opened his stupid mouth.

"Oh, my God, seriously?" Hannah said, nipping his retort in the bud. The words just slipped right out.

All three men looked at her.

She hadn't meant to interfere and knew she should apologize, but she didn't want to. Since she was standing near the green pickup, she walked around the bed to the driver's side and opened the door. Then she simply stared at Jasper and waited.

He blinked, clearly surprised, then glared.

If he wanted a staring match, game on. She was way better at it than anyone she knew.

Finally, he shuffled toward her, muttering curses the whole way. She maturely decided not to demonstrate that she was better at that, too. She stood back to let him climb into the pickup with its cracked vinyl seat. It was a toss-up as to whether he had yanked the door closed or she'd slammed it shut.

And then she scrambled out of the way real quick, because she damn well wasn't going to eat any more of his dust.

Once she was safe, she looked at Seth. At least he was smiling.

"I'm sorry," she said, moving closer. "I know I wasn't supposed to say anything."

"Nah, you deserved to let off some steam. That was relatively mild payback, all things considered."

"It wasn't about this morning." She watched the idiot speed down the driveway. "I didn't like him saying that about your dad. That was low." She looked at Seth. "I'm sorry he's sick."

"He's doing okay. We had a brief scare. Retiring and having less stress was all he needed."

They both turned at the sound of Murray's wheezing laugh. "Well, sonny boy," he said, looking at Seth, then Hannah with a nod. "You might've just met your match."

"Oh, hell, I figured that out the minute I met her."

"Hey." She gave him a mock glare, then thought a moment. "No, I like that."

Murray chuckled. "I reckon I'll see you when I see you," he said, with a sly grin aimed at Seth, then he turned toward the barn.

Seth looked up at the cloudless sky; the sun was already dipping toward the Rockies. "Let's go get something to eat."

"Where?"

"There's a steak house in Blackfoot Falls. And the diner is decent. Or we can go to Twin Creeks. A barbecue joint just opened."

Hannah hesitated, she'd hoped for a tour of the ranch.

"Did I hear someone say they were hungry?" Murray had made a U-turn. "I fixed some chili and cornbread for lunch. I got plenty left over."

"I'm sure you do," Seth muttered wryly. "I think we'll pass."

Hannah remembered what he'd said earlier, but she had a serious weakness for homemade cornbread. "Did you make the cornbread from scratch?"

Murray looked insulted. "It's my own special recipe."

"I'd love to try some." She glanced at Seth. "Do you mind?"

He studied her as if she were nuts; after all, he had warned her about Murray's fondness for peppers. Then shaking his head, Seth gestured toward the bunkhouse. "Go right ahead."

It wouldn't surprise her if Murray had thrown in jalapeños. Adding different ingredients like peppers and cheese had been a trend in Texas for some time. And while she generally preferred it plain, she'd sampled some very tasty jalapeño cornbread.

She followed Murray to the bunkhouse, ignoring the flicker of amusement on Seth's face as he walked alongside her. "We won't be long," she whispered low enough that Murray couldn't hear. She didn't mean to be rude, but Seth was probably hungry.

The bunkhouse kitchen was bigger and airier than she'd expected. "Wow, this is nice," she said, eyeing the cast iron Dutch oven sitting on the stove and copper pots hanging over a wood chopping block. "Bigger and better equipped than my kitchen, that's for sure."

"How about trying some of my chili with that cornbread?" Murray asked as he bustled about, pulling a foil-covered pan out of the oven, setting out a small crock of butter and utensils.

"No, thanks. I think we're going someplace for dinner." She glanced at Seth. He didn't say a word, just looked on with that same amused look on his face.

Murray brought down plates from the upper cabinets and then peeled back the foil. The cornbread was a yummy golden brown, and yep, Hannah saw small chunks of jalapeño and something else—tiny bits of something red. Paprika? Weird for cornbread. Cayenne maybe? Whatever it was, Murray hadn't been heavy-handed at all.

Ha. These Northerners didn't know what hot was.

A small corner piece was gone, and Murray proceeded to cut the rest of the pan into hefty-sized squares.

"Just give her a small piece," Seth told him.

Hannah rolled her eyes, but she noticed the older man's mischievous little grin. "Where are you from, Murray?"

"Born and bred right here in northern Montana." He cut a square the size of a brownie and handed it to her on a plate. "Go on, have a seat. Napkins are on the table."

Without a word, Seth poured a glass of water and set it on the Formica counter next to her. Then he folded his arms across his chest and watched her as if she was a TV special or something.

Hannah stayed right where she was and took a bite. It was pretty good, but definitely not what she'd call hot. Wusses. She glanced around searching for the crock of butter. It had been moved to the old oak table.

"What do you think?" Murray asked.

"It's delicious. Honestly, it's so moist I wouldn't put any butter on it but I'm assuming you churned it yourself?"

"You're darn tootin' I did. Ain't no other way to eat it."

Hannah grinned and took another bite as she walked over to the table. The first sting of heat hit her way at the back of her mouth. She swallowed and the burn followed the trail down her throat. Okay, that hadn't been expected. But it wasn't bad.

Aware Murray was keeping tabs on her, she bit off another piece and chewed.

Fire exploded in her mouth. So sudden, so violently, it seared her tongue, singed the insides of her cheeks and roared up into her nasal cavity.

"Holy shit!" Tears filled her eyes so quickly they nearly blinded her. "Shit. Shit. Shit." The countertop was a blur. Where the hell was the water? No. Milk. She needed…

A large hand grasped her wrist. She felt a cold glass being pressed against her palm. "Have you got it?" Seth asked. "This milk should help."

"Yes," she squeaked.

She gulped down as much as she could without choking. Tears slipped down her face. Just as she was about to rub her eyes, Seth stopped her. "Don't do that," he said. "Wash your hands first."

"Is she okay?" Murray asked, sounding concerned.

Hannah was too busy trying to cheat death to yell at him. Although, it wasn't his fault. She'd been warned. But had she listened?

"Come on," Seth said, taking her by her shoulders and steering her to the sink.

Alternately coughing and sniffling, she washed her hands and then dried them on a towel he gave her. "May I have a napkin, please?"

Murray brought over a whole stack. "Sorry, miss. Truly I am. I didn't think it was that hot."

Hannah managed a small laugh before snatching a napkin and turning away to blow her nose. God, even that burned.

"Want more milk?" Murray asked.

She shook her head.

"Time to hit the road." Seth grabbed two bottles of water off the shelf of an open pantry, then took her hand and held it all the way to the truck.

He opened her door, waited until she was nestled in the bucket seat, then passed her both waters and closed the door. By the time he walked around and slid behind the wheel, she'd downed half a bottle.

Her face felt hot and flushed, and as for her tongue, while it wasn't one big fireball, the embers were still smoldering. Even the back of her neck was clammy. And she didn't dare look at herself in the visor mirror. All her tinted moisturizer must've rubbed off by now, exposing every single detested freckle. "I was such an arrogant jerk."

Grinning, Seth started the engine. "I wouldn't go that far."

"I'm sure Murray will be laughing for a month."

"No, he feels badly. He knew I'd warned you, and I guess he figured you liked spicy food."

"You mean he took me for a kindred spirit instead of a moron."

"Your words, not mine," he said, with a little smile as he reversed.

Hannah laughed. "Okay, I deserved that too." She glanced back at the house and stable as they drove down the driveway. But she hid her disappointment over not getting to see everything.

"Look, you can come over again before you leave. What day is that, next Sunday?"

She nodded. "Murray said something about you never taking a day off."

"That's not—" He sighed. "It's summer, so you know

how it is on a ranch. And Clint's been busy making himself scarce, what with all the wedding plans."

Hannah grinned. "Don't you mean he's busy *with* the plans?"

"No, I meant he's been hiding out. Even going to auctions he doesn't need to just to dodge the *firing squad* as he calls it. If you ever meet my mom, that's not something you want to share with her."

"Got it." She took another big gulp, wishing her damn mouth would stop burning. "Actually I would like to come back," she said. "You know, if it works out."

"We'll make it work. Though there won't be all that much of interest, with you having grown up on a ranch."

"I shouldn't have told you that. It's pretty embarrassing how little I know about what goes on day-to-day."

"Do you want to know?"

She considered the question for a moment. "Yeah, actually, I do."

They came to the end of the driveway where it met the gravel road. He stopped the truck and put the gearshift in Neutral. Resting an arm on the top of the seat behind her shoulders, he shifted so that he partially faced her.

"All right then, before you leave Montana, we're going to make sure you have a solid understanding of Ranching 101." Smile lines fanned out from the corners of his eyes. Today they were the color of warm caramel.

They held her captive as he leaned toward her. Her heart thumped wildly. She moved a few inches closer. They were just about to kiss when she remembered…

"Wait. My mouth is still…" She slumped back. "I taste like chili peppers."

Blithely he slid his hand behind her neck. "I like a little heat now and then," he said, bringing her closer again.

Their lips touched. He angled his head and molded his

mouth to hers, his hand tangling in her hair. He drew the tip of his tongue across her lower lip and a different kind of warmth bloomed inside her chest and spread south. She let out a soft gasp and he took advantage of her parted lips. His tongue swept inside and caressed hers.

He froze. Pulled back abruptly.

"Son of a bitch." He grabbed the unopened bottle of water, twisted off the cap and guzzled half of it. A few drops clung to his chin. He wiped his mouth with the back of his wrist. "Shit."

Hannah blinked at him. "I'll try not to take that personally."

"Murray's insane." A flush crawled up Seth's throat into his face. "What the hell kind of peppers did he use?"

"I think those tiny red specks were the culprits." She took a sip of her water. "Did you see him eat any cornbread? I mean he practically had a whole pan left."

Seth shook his head and laughed. "That sneaky bastard. I wouldn't put it past him."

"Well, this completely sucks."

"Nope." He shifted out of Neutral. "I know just the thing to cool us off."

7

FIVE MINUTES LATER Seth almost missed the turnoff. He hadn't been to Pine Creek since the week before he'd left for college. He and a few buddies had brought a case of beer and a bottle of tequila. Ashlyn and Courtney had showed up with homemade cookies and bags of chips, and turned the night into a sendoff party. Seth had been the only one in their small circle to continue his education. The rest of the gang had made it through high school by the skin of their teeth.

"Can I ask you something?"

Seth figured he knew what was coming. His only surprise was that it had taken Hannah this long. "Why did Jasper want you to speak for everyone?"

Again, she'd done the unexpected. "First of all, the majority of the ranches around here are small, they run maybe a hundred head, just enough to feed themselves and bring in a little extra money. Like your parents' ranch, so you get the picture." Seth squinted at the dirt road up ahead. A fallen tree had been moved to the side but the encroaching underbrush was heavy.

"Something wrong?" Hannah asked, following his gaze.

"Nope. Anyway, those ranchers don't care about BLM

land. At least not enough to kick up a fuss. And if some of their cattle do *wander* over to public land, the government has turned a blind eye. If those ranchers show up to the meeting, it's only out of nosiness or because they were bullied."

"What about Jasper? Does he fall in that category?"

"He has a larger ranch, though nowhere near as big as the Sundance or the Whispering Pines. But guys like Jasper are worried because they've used public land for years. Some of them who don't have enough land of their own actually depend on it."

"So now they'll have to buy grazing permits?"

Seth nodded. "Or trim their herds."

"Are the permits expensive?"

"I have no idea what they cost. I'm staying out of that entire mess." He saw the huge aspen with its thick trunk and the spruce on the opposite side that marked which fork to take. "We're almost there," he murmured as he drove closer to the trees. The damn spruce had grown like crazy.

"Um, I don't see any restaurants around here."

"I told you we need to cool off first."

"It is pretty here," Hannah said. "I see a few orange wildflowers."

Seth nodded, more concerned with the width of the spruce that had narrowed the road. The branches would scratch his paint.

"I can't tell if you did it on purpose or not, but you didn't actually answer my question."

He had to think for a moment. "Right. You were wondering why Jasper wants me at the meeting," he said. "I guess because I have master's degrees in range science and agricultural economics."

Her brows went up and her eyes widened.

"Told you I was a geek," he said, grinning. "We might have to walk from here. It's not far."

"Wait. Wait. You can't just—" She glanced at his hand on the door handle. "Okay, let's walk."

They both got out of the truck. She didn't go any farther, but stared down at her feet. "Am I going to kill myself trying to walk in these sandals?"

"I hope not."

"Yeah, me, too," she said so seriously he almost laughed.

"Didn't you pack walking shoes?"

"Oh, that's right. Give me a sec."

She bent over into the backseat to rifle through her bag. There wasn't a snowball's chance in hell he could stop himself from staring at her shapely rear end. The hem of her shorts rode up, showing more leg. The white material stretched thin over her backside, and it was a sure bet she was wearing a thong.

His cock twitched.

"Okay." She straightened suddenly. "Almost there," she said, sitting at the edge of the seat as she exchanged her sandals for Nikes.

In less than a minute they were on the trail.

"I hope you didn't take offense to my reaction. In my job I fill a lot of different kinds of positions in a variety of industries, but I don't even know what range science means."

"Anything from rangeland ecology and ecosystem science to natural resource management. Agricultural economics has more to do with property rights and Federal rangeland policies."

"Okay, stop. You're making my head hurt. Jesus, should I be calling you Dr. Landers?"

"Hell, no," he said, snorting. "I didn't mind school, but I'd had enough of classrooms. And frankly, I got everything out of the program I need. A PhD wasn't going to help me."

"But you're not really using the degrees, are you?"

"Better watch where you're stepping." Slipping an arm around her waist, he steered her away from a ground squirrel burrow. He liked the way she fit against him and kept her right where she was against his side.

"Scratch that last question. I can't believe I asked. I'm constantly working with people who find themselves in the wrong career or are disillusioned about what they thought they wanted to do."

"My reason is simple. I like being a know-it-all," Seth said. "Just ask my brothers."

"Hmm. I just might. Are they as good-looking as you?"

"Of course not."

Hannah laughed, and he liked the open, carefree sound of it. It filled him with a lightness that he hadn't felt in a long time. He also liked her adventurous spirit. She hadn't nagged him to tell her where they were going. Just like last night. He'd said it was a surprise and she was content to leave it at that.

"I have more questions," she said, smiling up at him as they continued to walk.

"I'm sure you do." He could see the freckles across the bridge of her nose more clearly now, and he found himself counting them. Maybe a dozen or so, not many. He wasn't sure why he liked them so much.

"Last night you said something about being in the air force. Was that after college?"

"Yep. Six months after graduation. After I got out I went back to school for my masters."

"Were you an officer? I bet they went after you with both barrels."

Lowering his arm, he stopped. "Do I seem like officer material to you?"

"Honestly, I think so."

That stunned him. "I'm highly insulted."

"Hey, wait," she said, catching his arm when he started to continue on. "You can't hold that against me. I don't know you well enough."

"That's true." Even if he were pissed, looking into those pretty brown eyes, he would've forgiven her. "How's your mouth?"

"Not too bad. Yours?"

He bent to brush his lips across hers.

Hannah let out a soft sigh and placed a hand on his chest. "I hate to say it, but we'd better wait a bit longer before we dive into anything."

"Better to be safe, huh?"

"That's my motto."

He took her hand. "Come on."

"Wait. I'd like to defend myself."

"Against what?"

"What I said about you being officer material. You showed restraint with Jasper. You were rational, calm but assertive. And you could've easily justified kicking his ass. Instead, you even asked me not to say anything."

"You forgot a key factor. The ability to take orders."

"Did you have a problem with that? Because I don't—"

"No," he said, interrupting. The conversation wasn't going anywhere. "It's just that not all directives make sense. In the military you do things without questioning."

Hannah nodded, and they continued to walk. "I wasn't saying you should rethink a military career. Honestly, not my intention at all. In case I really did insult you, I wanted to explain."

"No worries."

"Why did you join the air force in the first place?"

"I was young and stupid. And needed to get away for a while."

"Were you tired of ranch life?"

"No." He exhaled the breath he'd been holding. "I got into a little trouble my junior year of college. My family didn't react all that well. Not that I blame them. Now, at least. Back then…" He shook his head.

They walked in silence for a while. He could hear the babbling water as it flowed through Landers land into the creek.

They were getting close.

"Was that when you got into trouble with Jasper?"

Seth smiled. "That was smooth," he said. She'd slid right into the question he'd expected from the very beginning. "Are you sure you're not a reporter?"

Her eyes widened. "I'm so used to interviewing people for my job I run on autopilot sometimes. You know what? That question was too personal. Don't answer."

He opened his mouth to tell her they were almost there…

"I mean it. Don't tell me."

"Okay." Laughing, he squeezed her hand and wondered how she was going to react to what he had in mind for them. He thought he knew, or he wouldn't have brought her here, but she did have a habit of surprising him.

They spent the next few minutes in the peaceful quiet of the leaves rustling in the trees and the crunch of dead brush and bark underfoot.

"I hear water," she whispered.

"Our town is called Twin Creeks," he said, as Pine Creek came into view. "This is where the two meet."

He helped her over a fallen log, and there was the big

flat rock that butted up to the watering hole. It was the only place for miles where you could actually take a dip, although it wasn't very deep.

"It's so clear," she said, picking up the pace to get to the water's edge. "I can see the pebbles. And a fish!" She pointed, her excitement making him grin.

"Yeah, people do plenty of fly fishing along these creeks further to the south. This little pond is on Landers land, and there's no reason for anyone to come poking around back here. So not very many people know it exists."

"It's gorgeous. Like something you'd see in a coffee table book. So many trees and the brilliant blue sky. This is amazing. I wish we'd brought a picnic."

"You're hungry. I promise we'll get food soon," he said, releasing her hand. "But first…"

"I'm really not—"

Seth walked over to the rock and stripped off his shirt.

"What are you—?" Her brows rose.

"The water's cool, and not very deep if that's a concern."

"I don't have a suit."

"Me, neither. No one's going to see us."

Her eyes had widened, making it easy to see the trail they followed down his chest, past his belt to where she stalled a few inches lower. "Oh."

"I suppose you could wear your underwear."

"I could," she said, briefly meeting his eyes before she looked south again.

To get the ball rolling, he undid his belt, his button, and his zipper.

After blinking several times, she grabbed the bottom of her tank top. "Oh, what the hell."

His hands paused as her bra came into view. It was

beige and lacy, and it made his mouth water to see what came next. But he didn't want to be an ass.

Just in time, he remembered to get his boots off before he dropped his jeans and boxer briefs. Careful to fold them, he set them on the rock, leaving his left pocket in easy reach.

When he looked over at Hannah again, her cheeks were pink, her smile tentative as her unhooked bra slipped from her body. It took his breath away, how beautiful her breasts were, round and full, with coral nipples standing out against her pale skin.

He knew she was getting an eyeful of him, as well. He'd been half hard, just knowing what they were going to do, but now the only way he was going to stop his growth spurt was to jump into the chilly water. Which he'd better do soon.

Luckily, she'd already peeled her shorts off, and as he watched, she hooked her thumbs under the sides of her lacy beige thong and pushed down.

She dropped the thong on top of the rest of her clothes and stood there with a perfect small V of trimmed brown hair and a blush spreading beyond her cheeks. Which got him moving again.

He didn't even stop to test the water temp, just kept on walking into the cold creek until he was waist deep. He only winced a little when the warmest parts of him felt the shock. It did the trick. He shrank like a…

"You okay?" Hannah asked, putting her clothes next to his.

Guess he hadn't been as stoic as he'd thought.

She didn't toe off her Nikes until she got to the edge of the creek. She dipped her toes in and yelped. "It's cold."

"All the better to cool us down," he said. "Trust me, it'll feel great in a few minutes."

"But first, I'd have to actually get in the water."

"That's true."

"But it's June. It shouldn't be cold."

"Spoken like a true flatlander." He didn't even pretend he wasn't enjoying the view. "Then again, take your time."

Having forgotten her embarrassment, at least for the moment, she shot him a look and laughed. "Turn around."

"Is that a joke? I have a gorgeous woman in front of me..."

"I'd do it for you."

"Go ahead, turn around then. I'd like that."

"Funny man." Shivering and rubbing her arms, she waded in up to midcalf.

"Hurry so we can rub up against each other. It'll keep you warm."

Hannah studied him for a few seconds. "Here's a fun fact—if you say gullible really slowly it sounds like oranges," she said, then like the trouper he'd thought she was, she walked straight on in.

8

AFTER HER TEETH stopped chattering, Hannah had to admit, he was right. Not about the water feeling great, that hadn't happened yet, but rubbing up against him? "Oh, yes," she said, running her hands over his slick back until she had one hand squarely on each cheek.

"Feels good, huh?"

"*You* feel good. For the record, I prefer my swimming holes to be the temperature of tepid tea."

"Now that doesn't sound like you at all."

"Why not?" She gave him a little pinch, just because.

"Ow. Because you're bold and adventurous." He had one hand busy on her right breast while the other meandered over her hip.

That wasn't completely true. She wasn't always this bold. Something about Seth seemed to make her brave. "Who says I have to freeze my ass off while being superwoman?" She kissed the grin right off him, then lightly nibbled his chin.

He moved his hand from her hip to her left butt cheek, and squeezed. "Nope, it's still here. Better check the other one."

"No," she said quickly, pressing against him, trapping his hand on her breast. Whatever he was doing to her nipple, she didn't want it to stop. "I'll concede. Both cheeks accounted for."

Seth smiled and swept the loose strands of hair away from her eyes. The water barely reached her breasts and only hit Seth at the bottom of his ribcage. She had to touch his chest. She'd been dying to feel the swells and contours of his pecs since last night when they'd sat snuggled together on the blanket.

She rested a hand on his shoulder, the rock-solid feel stopping her for a moment. But then she couldn't resist trailing her fingers along the cords of muscle, before expanding her exploration to his chest.

Tempted as she was to use both hands, in the light of day it seemed too greedy. So she made do with skimming her palm over the soft hair dusting the skin between his hard, dark nipples. She let two fingernails graze the right nub and he inhaled deeply.

She glanced up at him, just as he lowered his head and kissed her. It was a soft brush of his lips across hers, a light stroke of his tongue. Nothing like she'd expected. And then he deepened the kiss, distracting her while he slipped his fingers between her thighs.

Her gasp was one of surprise, nothing more, but Seth paused. So she gave him a little wiggle, which he figured out very quickly.

"Oh," she murmured, her lids fluttering closed as he rubbed her in exactly the right way. Almost of their own volition, her fingers trailed down to his hard belly. "Too bad we'll have to get out of the water soon," she said.

"Why's that?" He moved his mouth to the side of her neck.

"Lubrication."

"Hmm?"

"It won't last."

Popping upright, stilling his fingers, he looked startled. "Am I hurting you?"

"Not yet."

"But I might."

She scrunched her nose. "I'd tell you."

"Do you want to get out now? Or is the water starting to feel like a cup of tea?"

Thinking it over, the answer seemed very simple. "Both."

He took her hand and carefully led her to the shoreline, while she enjoyed the view in front of her. Why were men's butts so enticing? His was perfect. Muscular with those amazing cheek dimples that made the butterflies in her tummy swoop low.

When he turned, there was another surprise. And damn, her hand had been only inches away. "Well, you were clearly in the perfect temperature."

He smiled, not bothering to glance down. "What did you expect? You're gorgeous."

She blushed for about the hundredth time. "Funny, I was thinking the same thing about you," she said, her gaze snagged by the water dripping down his six pack. A few drops glistened off the smooth, taut skin of his cock.

His short laugh sounded a bit self-conscious.

She quickly turned around and tried to wring out her hair. Fortunately, only a couple of inches at the ends had gotten wet. Her luck ended there. Rocks and sharp twigs cut into the soles of her feet.

"Where are you going?"

"I need my—"

He came up behind her, wrapping his arms around her and kissing the side of her neck. "Is this what you need?" he whispered, and kissed her jaw, nibbled her earlobe, licked the skin sloping toward her shoulder. "Hmm, Hannah?"

"Yes," she said, held against his strong chest and getting lost in the moment, and then she remembered. "And my shoes."

Seth went still.

Then he laughed, the sound a pleasant rumble near her ear.

His chest shook against her back. "Where are they?"

She pointed. "Don't the rocks bother your feet? Some of them are sharp…"

Seth swept her up into his arms, startling a squeak out of her. Automatically her arms went around his neck as he carried her to the big flat rock close to her shoes. It was awkward for a few seconds, and she realized he was trying to evaluate the situation before setting her down on the smooth, warm surface.

"You could've just thrown me the shoes."

Lifting a brow, he gave her an amused look. "Don't you have any romance in your soul?"

"Um…is that a trick question?" She watched him turn and bend to pick up her Nikes, and she had to press her lips together to keep from grinning like a loon. "I was worried about you hurting your back."

"Here," he said, handing her the shoes. "I doubt you'll need them for a while."

She grinned then. He'd get no argument from her.

When he reached around her for his jeans, she almost whimpered in protest. But instead of putting them on, which would have crushed her into a gazillion pieces, he pulled a condom out of his pocket.

And two more tumbled out with it.

She laughed. "Optimistic, aren't you?"

"I hope for the best."

"I like that about you," she said, getting up to press her slightly chilly body against his.

He pulled her closer with one arm around her waist. "The rock seems warm."

"Hard, though."

"True."

She would have responded but he kissed her again, languid and sweet, the sound of the rippling creeks and chirping birds the perfect accompaniment. With barely any effort, or brambles under her bare feet, he switched their positions so the rock was behind him.

When he pulled away from their kiss, she let out an embarrassing sound, like a kid whose candy was taken away. But she saw it was only to take care of the condom business. Turned out that being an air force cowboy made one very adept with one's hands.

Then his attention was all on her again. "Come here, you," he said in a quiet, sexy tone that had her obediently stepping into his arms.

She sighed at the feel of his warmth and strength, his erection rubbing hotly against her hip. Seconds later, Hannah thought she heard something, or someone, moving in the trees behind them. She stiffened.

He pulled back to look at her. "What's wrong?"

"Could someone be watching us? I'm pretty sure I heard something."

After following her gaze to the dense grove of aspens, he lifted her chin until she met his eyes. "It's probably an animal. No one comes all the way out here."

"We did."

Seth smiled. "Touché," he said, stroking her back. "If you're uncomfortable or worried, we can leave."

"I don't really want to…" She glanced at the giant juniper edging out a struggling young aspen. Staying completely still and quiet, she just listened. Chirping insects and the sound of the creek water hitting the rocks as it flowed south, that's all she heard. "So, you don't think we have anything to worry about?"

"I don't, no. But it's more important that you feel comfortable."

"I trust your judgment," she said, and some odd emotion flickered in his eyes before he lowered his head.

He rolled his tongue over her nipple a few times before sucking the stiff peak into his mouth. Shifting, he leaned back against the rock and moved a hand underneath her right thigh, lifting it so it rested gently on top of his leg.

"I'd better check," he said. "About the whole lubrication thing."

"I don't think it's going to be a problem." She let her head fall to the nook of his shoulder as his fingers spread her once more.

"You really are gorgeous, you know that?" he whispered, stroking her back from neck to behind.

"Here I was just thinking I won the vacation jackpot."

"I'm the lucky one," he said, pushing his thick, hard cock inside her.

It was unexpected and so amazing, she bit him.

"Ow," he said, before he chuckled. "I knew I had to be careful with you."

"Accident. Sorry. Won't happen again."

"Did I say I didn't like it?"

She lifted her head, and even though it was getting more difficult to speak, she asked, "Do you—are you into any—"

"I'm insanely turned on."

She adjusted her raised leg and her hold on his neck, and between them, there was no more talking.

Panting. Moaning. A groan so low it made her ache.

Even nearly losing their balance didn't put a damper on anything.

He lifted her all the way up until both her legs were wrapped around him, and she moved the best she could, but mostly he did the work. Moving his hips, pulsing in and out. Groaning and pushing in harder when she squeezed her inner muscles around his cock.

Quivering inside, the pressure built so quickly she didn't have the wherewithal to slow it down, enjoy the sweet agony of teetering on the edge, of fighting off the tumble into sensual oblivion.

Unexpectedly, fantastically, the angle of his strokes was so excellent that she climaxed. Hard. Even though his hands were busy cupping her butt. Even though she was busy just hanging on to him.

Before the spasms had subsided, Seth moaned low in his throat. His body tensed. He kissed her hard and deep, and then he came, too.

A minute later she still hadn't caught her breath so verbal communication was out. She squirmed a little to remind him to let her down.

"You know what?" he asked, his breathing still ragged as he gently guided her down his damp body.

"What?"

"Not that this wasn't great," he said, "but this is kind of ridiculous."

"What? The acrobatics or that I think I stepped on a bug?"

"The fact that I have a perfectly decent bed back at the house. My folks are gone until Tuesday, Clint and Lila won't be back until late tonight, or even tomorrow. Think about it. A whole bedroom to ourselves. An attached bathroom with a shower and a tub."

"Food?"

"Lots."

Hannah used up her last reserved breath to give him a light shove. "Why didn't you say so earlier?"

SHE WAS GLAD Seth didn't park where they had before. Instead, he took the fork that led all the way to the house, which was even more impressive up close. She loved the porch with its two big rocking chairs. She imagined how nice it would be sitting out here having drinks at sunset and enjoying the view.

Having sex.

Damn, her brain needed a serious reboot. They'd had sex on a stupid rock, for God's sake. Outside. In broad daylight. In a less than ideal position. And yet it had been amazing.

She blinked, swallowed, all in the hope of clearing her thoughts. She glanced at Seth. The way he was watching her, his eyes five shades darker, didn't help. She was pretty sure he was thinking back to their little adventure.

Ordering herself to refocus, she climbed out of the truck, and they took the stone walkway together. Not touching. But almost.

The house itself was part ranch-style, part Alpine. Seth pushed open the door, and it surprised her how big the front room was. "Wow. This is…"

"Unexpected," Seth said, a smile in his voice. "It looks smaller from the outside."

She nodded, her gaze moving to the big stone fireplace. Even with the high ceiling, overstuffed chairs and homey little touches made the living room feel cozy. Of course, it was another really great place to—

Surely the pictures on the mantel would distract her. She walked over to investigate, and saw that almost all of the photos were of Seth and his brothers, some with them wearing sports jerseys and some with horses. Boys and horses. Trophies held high, ribbons worn with pride. There were some studio shots of the family at different stages and a couple of sweet photos of what looked like his parents and grandparents.

It was such a warm tableau it made her stomach clench. If it weren't for her own mother's insistence that they needed some pictures of Hannah, their mantel would have been bare. And the photos that were displayed all looked as if they'd been taken under duress. Which, she supposed, they had. But this family? This was the real deal.

"The place was built by my great-grandfather," Seth said, joining her at the fireplace. "But my granddad and my father added on to it. There's enough room for half a dozen hands, and you should see the basement. We've got enough supplies to last an entire Montana winter."

"Will Clint and Lila live here after they're married?"

"They're building a house about a mile from here."

"Well, I love it."

"I'm glad," he said, dropping his hat on an end table. "Let's go get something to eat."

The kitchen matched the rest of the house in scope, with double ovens and a huge six-burner stove with a vent the size of her walk-in closet at home. The island could easily handle four people all working at the same time.

"I can't even believe this place. It reminds me a little of the Sundance—I mean, because of the modern additions. I guess it's like this for a lot of the older ranches, since they go back so many generations."

"They're of a type," Seth said, already staring at the contents of the refrigerator. "They all have to accommodate large groups for work and meals. A big ranch runs on its stomach."

"So do I." She joined him, not at all surprised by the bounty before her. "Is that a smoked turkey leg?"

"And a wing, and half a breast." He pulled out a platter with the remains of what must've been a twenty-plus pounder. "My mom made coleslaw, which I highly recommend, and she always keeps vegetables ready to put together a salad."

"Salad seems too complicated. But that coleslaw sounds great."

"There might even be potato salad in there," he said, putting the turkey on the big island.

"Is there anything we shouldn't touch?"

"Nope. Go for it."

Shamelessly, she rifled through the contents of the second shelf until she found the potato salad, and because this was her lucky day, she also found the remnants of what looked like peach cobbler.

She took both of her finds with her to the island. "Ah, that stuff's great," he said, nodding at the dessert.

"Plates?"

While he reached into an upper cabinet, she ripped off part of the turkey leg and moaned with her first bite.

Seth choked out a laugh. "What was that?"

Too busy chewing, she took another strip of the dark meat and brought it to Seth's mouth when he joined her. He took it and sucked on the tip of her index finger. Setting down the plates, he put a hand on her waist.

"Soon," she said. "I need to make sure my stomach isn't the loudest part of us having sex."

He almost spit out the turkey. He got them each a fork, and she portioned out the accompaniments, but they both tacitly agreed that feeding each other was much more fun than minding their manners.

His hip was pushed up against the island, and she mirrored him, not caring anymore about the décor when she had him to ogle.

Dammit, the man even looked hot while he ate.

"I'm going to have to stop soon," she said.

"Why?"

"I don't want to fall into a food coma when there's something so much better to do."

"Good point." He leaned forward and kissed her with his juicy lips. The only problem with eating with their fingers was that messing around wouldn't be pretty. She wasn't sure she cared all that much.

What did make things come to a crashing halt was the knock on the kitchen door.

She sprang back from Seth as if they'd been caught stealing the family heirlooms.

His eyebrows dipped into a scowl. "Now what?"

He grabbed a napkin from the center of the island, wiped his mouth and went to open the door. Murray stood there with his hands in the pockets of his overalls.

"I told that boy not to bother you. Made it real plain. There ain't nothing you can do."

"What are you talking about?" Seth asked. "Told who not to bother me?"

"Paxton didn't call you?"

"Not since he wanted the key."

"Oh. I saw your truck and—" Murray leaned to the right. He looked at Hannah, then the food, then back at her.

"Hi, Murray." She got rid of her napkin and wiggled her fingers in a small wave. "I was hoping you'd brought us more of that yummy cornbread."

He wheezed a short laugh. But it was obvious even to her that something was wrong. "Never mind, it's nothing," he muttered to Seth, then he nodded at Hannah. "Sorry to disturb you."

"Wait," Seth said when he turned to leave. "What's going on, Murray?"

Hannah could hear the old man's sigh from halfway across the kitchen. "It's Matilda. She ain't doing so good. I'm keeping a close watch, though. If she don't get more comfortable in the next hour or so, we're gonna have to call Doc Yardley."

"Well, shit. You haven't seen any change?"

"Not as much as we expected. But you don't need to worry none. I know what to do. This ain't my first sick mare, son."

Seth didn't move for a few seconds, then he nodded. "Keep me posted, okay?"

"Will do."

Seth closed the door, then turned to her before he'd cleared the worry from his expression. She knew right then he wasn't going to be able to forget about the sick mare or his duty. But did she really expect anything less from him?

Damn, the man just kept doing things to steal another little piece of her heart.

Although his smile was valiant and his touch warm and gentle as he tugged her close, there was no getting past the facts of the matter.

"You know what?" she said, looking up at him.

"Hmm?"

"You should go."

"What? We haven't finished eating. And we haven't even made it to my bedroom yet."

"We've got a whole week, remember? And to tell you the truth, I'd rather we wait until the only thing on your mind is me."

"It's not my first sick mare, either," he said, leaning in to give her a very persuasive kiss. But when he pulled back, the concern was still in his eyes.

"Nope," she said. "Maybe you could run me back to the Sundance. Or someone else could, so you don't have to leave."

"Wait, wait. This is silly. Why don't we just go to the stable, let me check out the situation, then we'll decide what to do. For all I know, things are going to work themselves out in the next ten minutes."

"Let me put away the food," she said, knowing she wouldn't be staying. "Then we'll do just that."

9

AT NINE THIRTY the next morning, Hannah sat cross-legged in the middle of her bed, glad she'd given in and brought her tablet with her. She didn't consider herself a workaholic, but she did put in a lot of hours and she really meant for this week to be a vacation. Still, it wouldn't hurt to find out all she could about this grazing permit business.

For going on three years her dad had been struggling with the ranch. Never enough grass or water or fattened heifers to send to market. Sure, the permits and transporting the herd would cost. But it seemed a lot of money was already going out with little coming in, and there was no relief in sight. It would be foolish not to check into a possible solution. And if she did find the answer, how could her old man do anything but stand up and take notice?

She heard her phone and leaned toward the nightstand to see the text. Just as she thought, it was Seth. She'd heard from him an hour ago, letting her know the mare was on the mend. But poor Seth had stayed up with the horse most of the night and had only managed to grab a few hours' sleep. He was trying for a couple more now and would call her later.

None of it surprised her. She'd known the moment Murray had told Seth about the mare that he would do everything he could to make the horse comfortable, if not well. Even if it meant cutting their date short. Because that's the kind of man Seth was.

Granted, she barely knew him, but she'd learned if she paid attention, she could read a lot in a man's eyes. The gift, ability, whatever one called it, made her very good at her job.

Of course she'd been disappointed; she was only human. But had he ignored the ailing horse just for sex—even damn sensational sex—Hannah would've taken that five times harder.

Anyway, they planned to see each other later. And right now, she had a lot of homework to do. Who knew grazing permits could be such a volatile and complicated issue? After what she'd learned in the last hour, and not knowing where Rachel stood on the matter, Hannah was reluctant to ask her questions.

But she'd been staring at the screen, hopping from one website to another until her eyes were blurry and her head was spinning. No wonder Jasper wanted Seth to do the talking. Some of the language regarding property rights was absurdly confusing.

Seth was really the person she should talk to, but that was out of the question. He'd made his intention to stay out of the argument quite clear. And, honestly, after some of the vile, online comments that she'd read, she didn't blame him.

God. Had she managed to go even ten minutes without thinking of the man? Seth was very likely the best surprise she'd ever had in her whole life. Not counting her year-end bonus, given the fact it had provided most of the down payment on her new condo. But damn, Seth was a close second.

She reminded herself that she'd known him all of two days. Tomorrow he could do something annoying that she couldn't stand. But he had a nice, easygoing vibe about him that made her feel comfortable—and so relaxed, she'd even let him see her freckles. That was a pretty big deal for her.

Holy crap, she'd actually gone skinny-dipping. She almost wanted to tell Rachel. It was just too funny.

And last, though hardly least, the sex had been ridiculously hot and incredible, and would likely haunt her long after she left Montana. However, she did have something to be grateful for. She'd met Seth the first day of her vacation instead of toward the end. That was super lucky.

Hannah reached for the mug she'd set on the nightstand and was bummed to find she'd finished her coffee. The big decision now was whether to sneak to the kitchen for more or see if she could go back to sleep. She drew up her knees and tugged her nightshirt over them. She wouldn't hear from Seth for another couple of hours. And between thinking about him and her dad's ranch problems, her night had been far from restful.

This was so damn hard. Was it worth going to the town meeting tomorrow night? Maybe it would enlighten her. Help her decide whether or not doing more research was worth the effort.

It pissed her off that here she was, on vacation, halfway across the country from dusty West Texas and she still worried about her dad's problems. The stubborn jackass had probably created them himself.

Well, of course she knew he had nothing to do with the drought. Sighing, she rubbed her eyes. Why did she allow herself to be reduced to a twelve-year-old when it came to her dad? Trying to win him over was a losing proposition. He'd wanted a son, period. And since she didn't plan on undergoing a sex change operation any time soon, she might as well throw in the towel. Again.

And she would. This time for good. Right after she got a handle on the dozen-plus stipulations from health inspections to leasing the right kind of land. At least she'd verified that trucking the cattle to Montana wasn't over-the-top expensive.

Reaching for her coffee, she remembered the mug hadn't magically been refilled. She grabbed her phone, instead. Even though she was still in the discovery phase of this Hail Mary pass to help her dad, it would probably be good to let her folks know there might be a ray of hope.

She hit speed dial, then closed her eyes.

THERE WASN'T ENOUGH coffee in the world to make four hours of sleep feel like anything but torture. Especially after spending most of last night worried that the mare might not make it. Matilda was his mom's favorite horse.

Seth scrubbed a hand over his face. At least inside the stable it wasn't so damn bright.

"Well, you look like shit."

Seth eyed Clint, deciding whether he should comment or not. "Not" won.

"Hey, listen," his brother went on, as if he didn't know better. "I'm sorry I left you holding the bag. Matilda was fine before we left."

"She's okay now. Don't worry about it."

"It would've been hard for us to get home earlier, even if I'd known what was happening. We ended up going all the way to Butte looking for something Lila's mom wants for the centerpieces."

"It's fine," Seth said, amused and shaking his head.

"What?"

"That's a word I never thought I'd hear coming out of your mouth."

"What…centerpieces?" Clint couldn't repeat it without laughing. "I can't even get mad at Lila. She doesn't want all this hoopla, either."

"Oh, hell, you couldn't get mad at her if she set a lit match to your jeans."

"That's probably true."

"I still say you should elope."

"The other thing, Mom's having a good time doing some of the planning. With three boys she never thought she'd get a chance to do all this. I'm sorry it's dumping more work on you, though."

"No problem." Seth took another swig of his coffee, wondering if he should have brought a Thermos with him. Probably. But while Clint was in such a penitent mood… "I wanted to talk to you before we get too busy. I, uh, met somebody. And I was hoping we could work it out for me to take a couple days off. She's only here for a week, so, what do you think?"

Clint finished cinching his saddle, and turned to Seth. "You met somebody, huh?"

"Yeah. She's a friend of Rachel's, staying out at the Sundance." He went into the tack room and brought out his saddle and blanket, only to find Clint with a smirk on his face that told Seth everything he needed to know. "Let me guess—Murray?"

"You let her drive your truck, bro."

"Damn that old gossip. Did he tell you he almost killed her with his hot peppers?"

Clint chuckled. "Must've slipped his mind."

"So, can you get along without me?"

"No problem. You think I didn't take time off when I was getting to know Lila?"

Seth didn't say anything, just went back to get the bridle. Clint could've spat in his face, told him he didn't deserve any time off for the rest of his natural life. Not after the hell he'd put the family through. He owed them all so much, but Clint in particular. He'd carried most of the burden during Seth's long absences, spent simmering in anger and hurt.

"Now that I'm thinking about it," Clint said, "you taking some time off could work out well for me, too."

"How so?"

"For one thing I'm running out of places to hide. If I'm covering your workload I won't have time for wedding stuff. Hey, this girl, she know anything about wedding planning?"

"Her name's Hannah, and no. I already asked."

"Too bad. But still, you being gone is a great excuse. I know Lila wants to make her mom happy, but she still thinks I care about whether the bridesmaids wear lilac or purple. I don't even know the difference."

Seth smiled. "Glad to be of service."

"I also heard," Clint said, "that Parsons came by yesterday."

All Seth did was shake his head. The last thing he wanted to do was talk about that ass.

Clint got the message. "So here's the deal. I'm gonna need you this afternoon and for a while early tomorrow, because Joe and Paxton won't be done replacing fence posts, but after that, go ahead. Take a few days. Lila and I will be doing some painting at the house tonight, and the folks won't be home from Missoula until tomorrow night, so go for it."

"Thanks. I will. How's the house coming along?"

"Should be finished before the big day." Clint glanced toward the stalls. "Aren't you forgetting something?"

Seth jerked a look to his right, then turned all the way around. The blanket and saddle were sitting on the rail where he'd left them. "Shit."

He'd forgotten Orion.

The gelding whinnied from his stall way in the back, as if he'd run out of patience.

"Only staying a week, huh?" Clint said, grinning.

"Yep, just long enough," Seth muttered, and headed toward Orion. Long enough for what, though, that was the question.

IT WAS A CLEAR, bright Monday afternoon at the Sundance, but over the vast stretch of foothills between the ranch and the Rockies, the sky looked iffy. Lots of gray clouds. Occasionally the sun peeked out, but Hannah had the feeling the clouds would win in the end.

Rachel had just finished saddling her horse, and she and Hannah stood on the sidelines as Josh and Kyle, a pair of Sundance men, flirted with the guests while they readied the women's horses.

"What happens if it rains in the middle of the trail ride?" Hannah asked, glancing back to make sure she couldn't be overheard. "I can't imagine Kimberly and what's-her-name being okay with wet hair and smeared makeup."

"I doubt it'll be a problem. Most of those rain clouds are much closer to the mountains than you think. After we ride for a while, I'll decide if we should continue on or come back. But I always take ponchos and umbrellas, just in case."

Hannah would've loved to spend some time with Rachel, but she wasn't sure she wanted to do it on horseback, especially with a bunch of other women along for the ride. But Rachel had warned her when she'd booked the trip that the dude ranch was especially busy in the spring and summer.

"Damn, I wish I could get Jamie to take this group out," Rachel said. "But she really can't."

"I don't want to screw up your schedule," Hannah assured her. "I just figured I'd check if you had some time to spare. We have the rest of the week to catch up."

Rachel grinned. "Come with us on the ride. It won't be as nice as being by ourselves, but it could still be fun."

"You know I don't ride that well," Hannah muttered in a subdued voice, then realized her friend probably didn't know that at all.

"Really? Do you not like horses?"

"I adore them. I just can't ride very well."

Rachel studied her for a moment. "Your dad, right?"

"Yep." Hannah rocked back on her heels, feeling awkward suddenly. She didn't talk much about her dad. But back in college, there were times she'd confided in Rachel—typically after a visit home when her dad had been a bigger ass than usual. Just as he had been when she'd spoken with him earlier. The call had lasted all of two minutes and he'd still managed to piss her off. Prideful, condescending bastard. "Anyway, I'd probably hold you guys up."

"No, you wouldn't. Half these women had their first riding lesson yesterday. That's why I won't take them too far. It's kind of a beginners group."

Hannah sighed, trying to decide. Before the week was out she expected Seth might ask her to go for a ride with him. Maybe she should use this as a practice run.

"Look, no pressure, okay?" Rachel said. "Completely up to you, though you should probably decide in the next ten minutes so we can choose a horse for you. Now, tell me about Seth."

"I wondered how long it would take you to get around to him. You're off your game, girl."

"I know, right?"

Hannah laughed at her friend's troubled expression. "I don't think it's fatal."

"You don't understand…" Rachel paused long enough to nod at a man leading a horse from the back. "People around here depend on me for up-to-the-minute news."

Hannah studied her for several long seconds. "You know what's scary? I think you might be serious."

Grinning, Rachel didn't confirm or deny. "To be honest, I was surprised to see you this morning." She'd lowered her voice. "I figured you would've stayed out last night."

"That was the plan. Until Seth got a call." She gave a brief summary of yesterday's events, leaving out as much information as she provided. Though not because she didn't trust Rachel. They weren't kids anymore, and Hannah realized she didn't want to talk about herself and Seth like that.

On the other hand, she was incredibly tempted to ask Rachel what she'd meant about Seth *having issues*.

"Too bad your day was ruined. Seth's a good guy, isn't he?"

Hannah nodded. "It wasn't ruined. Not really. Hey, do you know Jasper Parsons?"

"Everyone in the tristate area knows that bigmouth. And now, with the BLM offering more grazing permits in the area, he's gone loco. Right along with his sidekick, Avery Phelps, who doesn't even raise cattle anymore. He just drinks."

"Rach, need another horse saddled?" The cute cowboy with the brown curly hair smiled at Hannah. She thought that was Kyle.

"Well, kiddo." Rachel was looking at her. "It's do or die time. What do you think?"

"Oh, shit," Hannah muttered. "We're probably looking at both. But what the hell?"

"Good for you." Rachel gave her a pretty damn hard slap on the back. "You should do a little riding every day until you leave. We'll just show your father."

"I'm not trying to prove anything to him. I'm done."

Rachel just smiled. Probably because she'd heard that before.

10

"Seth. Seth Landers."

He and Hannah were on their way to the steak house and had just climbed out of the truck when Seth heard his name. He glanced back and saw Sadie hurrying down the sidewalk toward them. Couldn't imagine what she wanted with him.

"Sadie's the mayor of Blackfoot Falls," he told Hannah, as they started walking to meet Sadie partway.

"She gets to wear jeans to work," Hannah said. "I'm so jealous."

They ended up convening in front of the *Salina Gazette* office.

"I can't believe I caught you here," Sadie said, slightly out of breath. She had to be in her fifties by now and slimmer than the last time he'd seen her. Mostly he'd known her as the owner of the Watering Hole. Her new city duties were probably keeping her active. "You hardly ever come to town."

"What can I do for you, mayor?"

"First, don't call me mayor." Sadie nodded at Hannah.

The women introduced themselves to each other before he could.

"Tomorrow night's meeting," Sadie said. "You're planning on coming, I hope."

Seth snorted a laugh. "That's the last place I'll be."

"I was afraid you'd say that."

"No offense, Sadie, but I don't even live in this county."

She shook her head. "It's not a Blackfoot Falls or a Salina County issue. Hell, I don't even have anything to do with the Feds. Or what they do with BLM land."

"So, why get involved? It's going to get sticky."

"That much I know. And that's why I'm asking all the big ranches to have a presence at the meeting so the smaller guys don't get bullied. I sure don't need to name names. We both know the pair of troublemakers I'm talking about."

"I thought the government rep was only coming to answer questions," Hannah said.

"That's the plan." Sadie sighed. "Assuming he can get a word in edgewise."

"What if you ask people for questions beforehand? That way you can prepare a list to be addressed and not open the floor until the very end."

Sadie laughed.

Seth couldn't help but smile. He hadn't expected Hannah to stay quiet. And in fact, her suggestion wasn't all that bad. For any other town where guys like Jasper and Avery didn't live.

"Oh, honey, please don't think I'm making fun of you. It's just that we've got some rowdy, stubborn characters around here that can't see reason even if it were to bite them in their behinds."

"She knows," Seth said, looking at Hannah. "She's already had a dose of Jasper Parsons."

"Oh, good Lord." Sadie shook her head. "I hope you know we aren't all batshit crazy."

"I'm an old friend of Rachel Gunderson, so, too late."

Sadie chuckled, then got serious. "Hey, that's an idea. I hadn't thought about Rachel. That girl won't take guff from anyone. I need to get her there tomorrow night. She'd help even things out."

"I'll come," Hannah said.

Seth stared at her.

"I mean, I think I might be useful even though I don't live here." She met Seth's eyes. "After all, I did get Mr. Parsons to shut up and leave the Whispering Pines."

"Well that's—"

"No." Seth cut Sadie off. "You don't want to get mixed up in that argument."

Hannah raised her brows at him. "I'm not planning to."

Ah, Christ.

He regretted his tone, his word choice, even before he'd seen that Hannah had very clearly taken offense. And she had every right to. "Look," he said, taking her hand. "I didn't mean to sound heavy-handed, I just—"

"Good." Hannah smiled.

Sadie tried hiding her amusement. She glanced over her shoulder and waved to a woman coming out of Abe's Variety Store.

"I just want to point out that you don't have a lot of time left here and is that really how you want to spend tomorrow evening?"

Hannah blinked.

Before she could answer, Sadie jumped in. "For what it's worth, I got Cole McAllister's assurance he'll be there. And Nathan, too."

"My brother?" Seth asked, shocked.

"Yep. Promised he and Woody would both come. I

haven't heard back from the Circle K or Ben Wolf yet. Ben's not really a cattleman. He mostly trains horses for those Hollywood folks, but a lot of the men here don't want to piss him off. If they've got a special animal the movie people are looking for, Ben throws the business their way."

Seth was still trying to figure out why Nathan would bother showing up. And bring his foreman, too? Woody likely wanted to come out of sheer nosiness. He and Murray were good friends. Go figure.

"Look, Seth, I won't pressure you. I understand if you want to stay clear." Sadie took a step back. "But I can say this, just like I told Cole and Nathan, I don't expect any of you to speak if you don't want to. Just showing your faces might give the bullies second thoughts. Should make the smaller ranchers feel more at ease. Think about it, that's all I ask." Sadie nodded at Hannah. "Nice meeting you. Maybe I'll see you tomorrow night."

"Maybe," Hannah said, and he hoped like hell she was just saying that to be polite.

But damned if he was going to say anything and stick his foot in it again.

TWO HOURS LATER the evening hadn't improved by much. He should have turned his damn cell phone off. No, that was downright crazy. Proof he wasn't thinking all that straight. Not getting the call could've led to things far worse than putting a damper on their dinner out. Like him getting caught with his pants down, literally, by his parents.

Seth shuddered at the thought.

Goddamn it. He'd had plans for tonight. Plans that included Hannah and him and his king-sized bed. Hell, he'd even changed the sheets three days ahead of schedule.

"But they're okay, right?" Hannah got into the truck with a little help from him, but when he got behind the wheel, instead of starting the engine, he stared at her.

"What?" She stared back. "They're just coming home a day early."

"Just?" Didn't she understand what that meant? Or did she not care? Still tired from staying up with Matilda most of last night, he was probably being overly touchy.

She blinked. "Wait. A day early? That means..."

"Tonight." He looked at his wristwatch. "They'll be home in two hours."

"Nooo." Hannah's shoulders slumped. "They can't do that."

"It's their house. They can do whatever they want," he said with a short laugh. Her whining actually made him feel better.

She sighed. "Why did I have that piece of pie? I was perfectly content after polishing off the chef's salad, and then somehow I was led down an evil road and succumbed to my one weakness."

Seth frowned, struggling to make a connection. "Okay. I have no idea what that has to do with our predicament," he said. "Wait a minute. I hope you're not thinking about running over for a quickie. We did that yesterday." He gently stroked her cheek. "I want to do it right this time."

"Me, too. Though, honestly, sex didn't even cross my mind." She gave him a soft look. "I was wondering how I'm going to get more peach cobbler."

He noticed a slight quiver at the corner of her mouth and lowered his hand. "Glad you can joke at a time like this."

"Only because you're so adorable," she said, cutting loose the grin. The next second it was gone. "I'm disappointed, too. Absolutely I am." She leaned over, took hold of his jaw and held him steady while she looked into his eyes. "But you're also dead tired."

Seth stared back at her. "*Pie* is your one weakness?"

She laughed. "Okay. You caught me." She released him. "I admit I also get a little weak-kneed when it comes to a certain Montana cowboy."

He stopped her before she settled back in her seat. And kissed her, hoping to get a hint of huckleberry from her lips. He wasn't disappointed. "You came at the right time of year."

"So I understand. I'm thinking your state fruit is huckleberry, from the way everyone from the waitress to the nosy couple at the next booth went on."

"Well, they were right, weren't they?"

She grinned. "Yes, okay. I'm going to do my best to have a slice every day that I'm here."

"I'll do everything I can to help you reach your goal. But now, I'm afraid I have to take you back to the Sundance."

Hannah sighed. "Okay. I understand."

Seth had been ready to turn the key. Instead, he leaned back, trying to think of an alternative. But she was right, he was pretty damn tired. Nothing registered. Except for the motel and he still wasn't sure how he felt about that. Especially since Hannah hadn't brought it up, either.

"I know what we can do," she said, straightening, a streetlamp catching the sparkle in her eyes. "You could sneak me into your bedroom now, before they get home. I won't make a peep. They won't even know I'm there."

He lifted a brow at her. "Is this about the cobbler?"

Conspicuously crossing her fingers, she shook her head.

"Yeah, don't worry about my ego," he said. "Anyway, you make a hell of a lot more noise than a peep."

Her slow grin made him want to break the speed limit all the way back to the Whispering Pines.

"Seriously, let's think about this. You have to get up at what, six?"

It was his turn to sigh. "Five."

"Why?"

"I need to help Clint move the calf house from the south field."

She nodded as if she understood. "And how long will it take?"

"Till around ten or eleven. Unless we encounter a problem."

"Huh."

"You wouldn't have your car, either, and trust me on this, you wouldn't enjoy following me around that early in the morning."

"Yeah, we should probably just take me home."

With considerable reluctance he finally got them moving, and by the time they arrived at the Sundance, he'd gone through a couple more scenarios of how they could still spend the night together. But it was no use. Both situations would end with them dead tired.

It finally occurred to him that he hadn't told her about the surprise he'd been saving. If his folks' call hadn't thrown him for a loop, he would've told her by now.

"You know," Hannah said, "you could come up to my room, spend the night, then go back to the Whispering Pines in the morning. When I get up at a human hour, I'll drive the rental over and join you. What about that?"

After making sure they'd parked off to the side so they wouldn't be bothered by anyone, he unbuckled his seat belt and turned to Hannah. "That could work. Fair warning, though, I'll have to leave by four fifteen."

"Goody," she said, leaning over to kiss him, but she

paused midway. "Not that you have to get up early." She sank back. "Oh, my God, that's like really insane."

He smiled at her in the dim light, remembering in torturous detail exactly what she'd looked like walking out of the creek, water glistening as it skimmed over her pale, naked breasts.

"Now, come here." Pulling her as close as he could, he made the most of those pouty lips.

Jesus, she woke up the fire inside him like a match to month-old hay. He couldn't remember the last time he'd been this attracted to a woman.

It helped that she seemed to be as eager as he was to touch everything within reach. It got even better when he slid a hand under her top and felt her silky skin.

She moaned, and that made his jeans too snug. And when she took charge of the gentle kisses and turned the heat up to scorching, he moved his hand to cup her breast.

It felt like only minutes, but it had to have been longer when they finally parted just enough to breathe. "Why is it that we keep forgetting there's a room available?" He tucked a lock of hair behind her ear. "Where are you staying? Is there a separate guest quarters?"

"Yep." Hannah wrinkled her nose. "But I'm staying on the same floor as the McAllisters."

Well, shit.

Hell, he shouldn't care if anyone saw him.

"But we're not going to do this." She put a silencing finger on his lips. "I'd love for you to spend the night with me. But not after you had so little sleep last night, plus having to get up with the chickens tomorrow…"

"Hey, I used do that in college all the time."

She nodded. "Mrs. McAllister's bedroom is next to mine."

Seth tried not to groan. Or look like a guilty teenager.

Hannah smiled. "Look, I can see how tired you are, and it's not even safe for you to be driving let alone handling ranch equipment. You'll just make me worry." She put a hand on his chest. "Let's make plans to see each other after you're finished with work tomorrow. Okay?"

He muttered a curse, not used to having to worry about this kind of shit. Until moving back last December, and with the exception of his stint in the air force, he'd lived on his own. "Well, can we at least make out for a while?"

Hannah laughed. "Yes, if you stop being a grump."

"What do you expect? The damn universe is conspiring against us," he said, as he reclaimed the territory under her top and reached around to the back of her bra. Her laughter made it harder for him to undo the clasp, but he managed. "I have a lot of catching up to do. A lot more places to explore." He bit gently on her lobe, then whispered into her ear, "I don't even know what you taste like."

"You've been kissing me all evening."

"Not what I meant."

"Oh," she said, and the giggling stopped.

He palmed her bare breast.

Her shiver made the nipple between his fingers even harder.

Surprisingly, she pulled his hand away, but he quickly realized why. "Does your seat go back any further?"

"No, but the steering wheel goes up."

"Hurry and put it in gear, cowboy. I'm getting ready to climb aboard."

He doubted he'd ever moved faster, clearing the way for her to climb over the damn center console to settle her knees on either side of his hips.

It was a tight fit. Perfect.

They came together in a kiss that rocked the truck, and

when she started undulating her hips against his cock, she wasn't the only one who moaned out loud.

It might've been uncomfortable if it wasn't so goddamn hot. Twice he thought about telling her to cool it, but the words never made it to his mouth. Which was busy leaving damp trails down her throat, on the sensitive spot behind her ear, just under her neckline.

"I haven't come in my jeans since I was fifteen," he said, not sure he was crazy about doing it now.

"Well, we did go skinny-dipping, and now we're making out in your truck with a whole bunch of people in the near vicinity. Coming in your jeans seems appropriate, don't you think?"

He didn't realize what she'd said for a minute, seeing as how he was kissing her neck and playing with a nipple. Plus, she was still gyrating. Then it hit him. He let go of her breast and gripped her hips, and she stopped moving. "What people?"

"That's okay, we're safe. The windows are fogged."

Seth exhaled and laughed at the same time. Glancing to his left, he saw that she wasn't wrong about the windows. "Was anyone watching?"

"I hope not." She smiled and did a slight shimmy.

Jesus. He was never going to survive the night. "Did I mention I have a surprise for you?"

"No." She licked his chin. "What is it?"

"I worked it out with Clint. I'll be taking some time off."

She sat as far back as she could and looked at him through the dim glow of the security light coming from the stable. "Really?"

He nodded. "You can still drive out tomorrow if you want…"

"What time is it, anyway?"

He pressed the button on his watch to illuminate the dial. "Shit." How was it possible? "It's quarter to ten."

"What?" She started to climb off, but her knee hit him too damn close for comfort, and then she jabbed herself in the middle of her back. Thankfully, she made it to her seat in one piece. "You need to go. Right now. And tomorrow, the minute you're finished doing whatever with Clint, you need to call me."

"Right," he said, wondering if he would be able to walk her to the door with his erection pressing so hard against his fly. He blinked a few times, feeling like he was in some kind of weird trance. But he wasn't about to just shove her out the door. "Let's go. Don't forget your bag."

He hadn't realized just how fogged the windows were until he got out. Upon closer inspection he saw they hadn't exactly been in their own secret love nest.

Hannah burst out laughing on the other side of the truck. "We had visitors."

"I know."

"No, I mean the up-close-and-personal kind."

"I know," he repeated, staring at the back window where someone had written *Get a Room* in the light coating of dust from yesterday's excursion.

"Someone wrote something on my window," Hannah said. "It looks like *wowzah!* I think."

Seth wasn't about to look around and give the culprits any satisfaction.

Hannah joined him on his side of the truck. "You don't have to walk me to the door," she said. "I'd rather you get home as soon as possible."

"But how about a last kiss?"

"Here? Now?"

"Why not?" He shrugged. "Since everyone in Northern Montana seems to know our business."

Without hesitation she dropped her bag on the gravel and slid her arms around his neck.

By the time he actually left, it was 10:34.

11

HANNAH STOOD OUTSIDE the Cake Whisperer waiting for Seth to arrive for the meeting. When they'd last spoken that morning, she'd told him she'd ride into town with Rachel, but at the last minute she'd decided to drive her rental. It would free them both up the following morning, since they hadn't planned that far ahead.

Since Clint couldn't come to the meeting and Nathan would be there, Seth had reluctantly agreed to attend. He might have been influenced by her mention of the motel. Which, in hindsight, was a mixed blessing. Not that she wasn't thrilled about spending the night with him. God, she couldn't wait. But it would have been easier to ask her questions about grazing permits if he wasn't present.

Kylie, the owner of the bakery, opened the door for a young woman wearing an apron from the local market. She handed her a white cardboard box, then turned to Hannah. "Still waiting, huh?"

She nodded. "I think I see his truck…"

She and Kylie had briefly met ten minutes ago when Hannah had pulled into town. The meeting was being held two doors down, and after it was over Kylie planned on opening the bakery for an hour. They joked about all the people who'd be looking for sugar fixes, although it wasn't really funny. Judging by the waves of people entering the meeting room, it seemed tensions were already running high.

"Have fun," Kylie said, as she ducked back into her shop.

Stepping to the edge of the curb, Hannah tried to figure out if that really was Seth's truck. You could sure tell this was cowboy country. Lots of trucks with lots of hunting rifles mounted in their back windows. Seth didn't have a rifle, though, and she was glad about that.

"Hey, darlin', you looking for a good time?"

At the sound of his voice, she grinned and spun around to face him. Thank God he was in a decent mood. "I wasn't sure you were coming. Rachel is saving us seats."

"I said I'd show up." Sadly, his smile vanished. He didn't want to be here, and she had a feeling this was more for her than Sadie. Hannah hoped it wasn't a mistake. "I had to stop and pick something up," he said, tugging her closer to the building as he pulled something out of his jeans pocket. "Know what this is?"

She stared at the key card, smiling so big she was lucky her face didn't crack. "The key to happiness?"

"And success."

"Oh, God, don't you dare jinx it."

"Right. Don't wanna do that."

Jeez, she sincerely hoped everything went smoothly. The meeting, their first slumber party. A grouchy-looking old timer shouldered past them and nodded at Seth with a look of surprise.

"Let's go inside before Rachel has to give up our seats," Hannah murmured, and led the way.

Five minutes into the meeting, after the mayor had introduced the surprisingly young and good-looking Rick

Sherwood from the US Bureau of Land Management, poor Sadie started to lose control of the agenda. Hannah quickly discovered the woman needed no sympathy. She had grit. Raising her voice a couple times subdued most of the audience.

People were still wandering in while the speaker explained about old and new regulations for grazing permits, and eventually it was standing room only. Hannah was sitting between Rachel and Seth, but she wished she'd thought out the logistics.

It was generally too noisy to tape the proceedings, especially once the floor was opened for twenty minutes of questions. So she was trying to discreetly type notes into her phone, and occasionally jotted down a word or two on a crumpled paper napkin she'd found in her purse.

While it had begun civilly enough, with Mr. Sherwood assuring the locals that if their property bordered BLM land, they'd be given priority to purchase permits, Jasper was the first to cause dissention. He demanded to know why, since his family had been there for four generations, he wasn't going to get a discount on the newly raised price.

That caused a lot of chatter around the room.

"What an ass," Rachel leaned over and whispered. "He's been cheating the government by grazing for free for forty years. They ought to back charge him with interest."

So far Seth hadn't said a word, but she could feel his tension every time Jasper or his buddy, Avery, asked a stupid question or tried to swing the discussion to "the government's overreach" in regard to range and water rights. Neither topic had anything to do with grazing permits. It was obvious they were trying to incite their neighbors. And each time the question invariably ended in a rant, the two men slid damning looks at Seth.

Rachel was almost as agitated as Seth, although she was less stoic. "Oh, for God's sake," she said, rising to her feet a second after Jasper stood yet again. "You've asked about the sovereignty of Montana three times now, Jasper Parsons, and it still has nothing to do with tonight's agenda, so why don't you sit down and be quiet."

He glared at her, his face nearly scarlet, and remained on his feet. "Maybe if Seth Landers would get off his backside and stand up for his neighbors' rights, I wouldn't have to keep asking."

A woman standing by the door called out, "Yeah, come on Seth. I heard you know all about that kind of stuff from college"

Seth's whole body tightened noticeably, but all he did was shake his head. "Just observing," he said, his jaw so tight Hannah worried he'd crack a tooth.

Jasper, filled with new vigor as someone else prodded Seth, pointed straight at him. "You're the one should be telling this government mouthpiece why families who've lived here since before Montana was a state ought not be forced to buy grazing rights from the feds."

"No one's forcing you to do a damn thing, Jasper," said a woman in the front row.

"I wasn't talking to you, Charlene," he grumbled.

Rachel stood and planted a hand on her hip. "Okay, Jasper. That's enough. Do I have to come sit next to you?" she asked, getting a laugh out of half the audience.

Parsons glared at her, but he sat down. Not that he was happy about it.

Hannah quickly rose to her feet. "Do grazing fees include the water used by the cattle? And if not, how many gallons are required for a herd of, say, a hundred head in a month?"

Several groans floated above the crowd as the clock was ticking down to the wire, but Mr. Sherwood jumped in with gusto to answer her question. And somehow managed to tie in the difference between livestock use permits and term grazing permits.

She'd actually wanted to know the answers to her two questions, but she was just as gratified that Seth's breathing settled, and while he wasn't exactly relaxed, he no longer seemed ready to combust, either.

Thankfully, at the end of Sherwood's lengthy explanation, Sadie stood, and called the meeting to an official close.

The second the gavel hit the podium Seth got to his feet, and Hannah and the rest of the group—Nathan, Rachel and Woody—joined him. Unfortunately, they didn't make a clean getaway.

Jasper got right up into Seth's face. Hannah was ready to bop him in the nose, and from the way Nathan and Rachel pressed in, she wasn't the only one.

"Why the hell aren't you standing up for us?" Jasper asked, his voice as ugly as his vicious glare. "Your family's been here as long as anyone's. We got rights. That government stooge acted like we don't have any at all. And you let him walk all over us."

"It's not the government's job to explain your property rights to you or anyone else." Seth's tone was low and fierce.

"And you're okay with that?"

"It doesn't matter what my opinion is. We're talking about the law. That's why I told you to hire a damn attorney. Now stand aside."

When Jasper's hands bunched into fists and he didn't

budge, Nathan stepped between him and Seth. "Come on, bro. Let me buy you and Hannah a beer at the Full Moon. I don't believe you've been there yet, have you?"

Rachel got real close, too.

Her brother, Cole, who'd come in late, joined them, subtly forcing Rachel to step back. Then he looked at Jasper. "Why don't you go find someone who wants to listen to your bullshit?"

Seth, Nathan and Cole were all well over six feet. The stupid little man finally showed some sense and backed off. Woody, who didn't have an inch on Jasper, made sure the idiot kept backing up.

While the others were focused on Jasper, Hannah slipped her fingers between Seth's. "Let's go with Nathan and Woody, huh?" she said, her voice soft, meant only for him.

She could see he was on the fence and wondered if any surly meeting attendees would be at the bar. He didn't need anyone popping off at him.

Although, clearly, they'd have to go through his big brother first. And her, Hannah thought, even though she knew Seth could take care of himself. But she hoped having a beer and maybe doing some venting might help relax him.

"Good to see you, Cole. It's been a long time," Nathan said, and the two men shook hands. "How about you and Rachel join us for a beer? I'm buying."

"Wish I could," Rachel said, sighing.

"Got a lot going on at the Sundance," Cole said, shaking his head. "Though let's make sure we all get together soon, huh?" His gaze included all of them, and Seth smiled a little but he still hadn't said anything.

While goodbyes were exchanged, Hannah studied Seth. She felt horribly guilty for nudging him to come, and for not telling him about what she was up to. But what was the chance anything would come of her digging, anyway? Her dad liked doing things the hard way.

"How about we go for just one?" she asked softly.

Seth met her eyes and smiled. "All right. Just one, though." He slid an arm around her shoulders and kissed her hair.

Nathan's brows shot up so fast it was almost comical. His gaze flew to his foreman. Woody shrugged and led the pack to the Full Moon.

The place was big, over two times the size of the Watering Hole. Country music poured out of the corner jukebox. In the back she could see pool tables, and in the middle was a dance floor. She didn't notice the stage at first. According to the sign on the wall, a band played three nights a week.

Nathan chose a relatively private corner table close to the front window. The glass was frosted, so you couldn't really see out or look inside, which was probably the point.

"The place looks nice. Clint mentioned something about a mechanical bull in the back," Nathan said, after the waitress had come and taken their order.

"Yeah, I heard." Seth leaned back in his chair trying to have a look. "Did he try it?"

"Nah. Well, if he did, he didn't say."

"You mean if he fell on his ass he wouldn't have told ya." Woody started to laugh, then shot her a look. "Sorry for the language, miss."

Hannah just smiled.

Seth gave her a one-armed hug and laughed. "She's heard it all before, Woody."

"So, Hannah," Nathan said casually. "Do you live around here?"

She was about to answer when Seth beat her to it.

"Hannah's from Dallas. She's a friend of Rachel's and she's staying at the Sundance. For four more days. So, I'm sure you understand why I don't particularly want to sit here looking at your two mugs all night."

Both men laughed. "Can't say that I blame you," Nathan said, and waved to someone across the bar.

He had the same dark hair as Seth, though Nathan wore his shorter. They had similar lean, muscular frames, and so did Clint, now that she thought about it. Although all she'd seen were pictures of him in his teens.

"Anybody know if they serve food here?" Woody asked, scanning the tables around them.

Hannah shrugged, and Seth shook his head.

"We'll ask the waitress," Nathan said, glancing toward the back. "It's not a bad place. I'm kind of surprised you haven't been here before, Seth."

"Haven't had time. Spring came early, so we've been just as busy as I'm sure you all have."

"I figured you might be keeping your head down," Nathan said, studying his brother. "People still counting your drinks?"

Seth blinked.

Hannah felt a spike of tension.

"As if they got nothing better to do," Woody said. "Damn busybodies."

Seth and his brother exchanged faint smiles. It seemed to relax Seth. And helped Hannah chill somewhat.

After a brief silence, Nathan's gaze flickered to her, then back to Seth. "I apologize if I spoke out of turn."

"Nah," Seth said, shrugging. "It's fine." He rested an arm along the back of her chair and toyed with her hair. "I went to college in Billings. Some buddies and I drove up here for a weekend. First night home I got arrested for a DUI."

His casual admission startled Hannah. "Oh," was all she could think to say. Then she dazzled everyone with her brilliance by adding, "How sucky."

"Guess whose equipment shed the car crashed into?" Seth looked slightly amused, which she didn't understand at all.

She thought for a moment. "Oh, no. Jasper's?"

The waitress arrived with their beers. As she set down the ice-cold mugs, Woody asked about food. Hannah didn't hear the reply, she was thinking back to their skinny-dipping adventure when Seth had mentioned he'd gotten into some trouble.

"You can't leave it like that," Woody said to Seth. "Tell her the rest."

Seth took a sip of his beer first. "Four of us used to take turns being the designated driver. Bobby, who was supposed to be it that night, had been drinking at the party we'd just left. He was on a football scholarship, which he could've lost if he was convicted of a DUI. So he convinced me to switch places with him." Seth shook his head. "I wasn't really that drunk, so I should've known better. When the deputy got there, I registered slightly over the legal limit, so I spent the weekend in jail."

"Is there a conviction on your record?"

"No. The judge reduced the charge to reckless driving. I'm sure it helped that he knew my family and I'd never been in trouble before. And me being barely over the limit probably counted for something, too."

"Hell, you were one of the smartest students who ever graduated from Twin Creeks High," Woody said proudly. "That couldn't have hurt none, either."

"Yet stupid enough to take the rap for his buddy," Nathan pointed out with a shake of his head.

To Hannah's relief, Seth took it well. In fact, he and his brother both laughed.

"Wait. Did you ever tell anyone you weren't the driver? Like the judge?"

Seth slowly shook his head, took another sip of beer. "In hindsight I should have," he said quietly, his tone taking a melancholy turn.

"Mr. Brilliant here only told the family a few months ago." Nathan bumped Seth's arm with his elbow.

"Okay," Seth said. "This conversation has run its course. Let's drop it."

He managed a faint smile but Hannah got the distinct impression he regretted saying anything.

The waitress stopped and set down a small bowl of pretzels, then grinned at Woody's forlorn look. "Sorry, honey, that's all we got," she said, then patted his shoulder and moved on.

"We'll grab a meal at the diner, then take home something for Beth." Smiling, Nathan glanced at his watch. "We should make it home before her post dinner feeding time."

"How is Beth?" Seth asked, then glanced at Hannah. "His wife. She's pregnant."

Assuming they were talking about a horse, Hannah let out a laugh. Then she couldn't help smiling along with Nathan. The fondness in his expression was just so sweet.

"What I wanna know is who the hell you are, little girl."

The loud slurred voice came from behind, startling Hannah.

"Speaking of lushes," Nathan muttered, as she glanced back. "Too bad a year in jail didn't teach him a lesson."

It was Avery, Jasper's partner in annoyance. "I saw you taking them damn notes," he said, staring straight at her as he wobbled a few feet away. "You a reporter?"

Nathan scowled at the man. "Get out of here, Avery."

"Go home and sleep it off," Seth added, tightening his arm around her shoulders.

"Or mebbe you're one of them government spies."

"Yep, that's it," Hannah said. "You found me out. Mind spelling your name for my report?"

"So, you're confessing?" Spittle spewed from the old man's mouth.

"Look, if you miss your jail cell," Nathan said, "I'm sure a drunk and disorderly charge will give you a night to get reacquainted."

Avery glared at him, then at Hannah.

Seth pushed back his chair. "Be happy to escort you to the sheriff's office."

Hannah clutched his arm. "I won't goad him anymore. He'll stop."

The man's loud belch nearly sent his thin frame toppling over. He turned around, muttering curses while weaving his way back toward the bar.

Seth took another pull of beer. "I don't remember him being this obnoxious. What was he locked up for?"

"Theft. After his wife passed he was in a bad way— drunk every night, stealing things, just so he could blame it on the Sundance guests."

"Too bad," Seth said quietly.

Woody snorted. "Woulda been easier to feel sorry for him if he'd treated the woman with some decency when she was alive."

After a minute of silence, Seth turned to Hannah. "Well, I think I've had enough fun for one night. How about you?"

"I'm ready." She searched his eyes for a gleam, a smile, any hint that their night hadn't been ruined. Giving up, she looked at Nathan and Woody. "Thanks for the beer, and I'm so glad I got to meet you. Despite the circumstances."

"Thanks, bro, and tell Beth I'll come by to see her next week," Seth added, getting to his feet. "Woody, I hope you get something in your belly soon. I can hear it rumbling from here."

He didn't take her hand. Not as they left the table or once they were outside on the sidewalk. She hoped it had nothing to do with anything she'd done or said. But she had the most awful feeling in the pit of her stomach.

12

"WHERE DID YOU PARK?" Seth asked.

"Nowhere near your truck, of course." She jerked her thumb in the opposite direction.

He smiled and shoved his hands into his pockets as they started to walk. She almost told him he didn't have to escort her, that they could meet at the motel, but it felt like a good opportunity to lift his mood. And find out if she'd done anything wrong.

As they headed for her rental, she sent him quick glances. "I'm sorry the conversation got so personal," she began, his pain and regret nearly as tangible as his arm brushing hers.

Seth shrugged. "It's okay. It's better now that we can talk about it and laugh."

"Thank God you had an understanding judge."

He didn't say anything for a minute. "He gave me forty hours of community service along with the fine, which wasn't bad, considering. But that wasn't the worst of it. Jasper, that bastard, made out as if his loss was huge. That old shed of his had one piece of decent equipment that was damaged and the rest was nothing but junk, but my parents ended up paying through the nose."

"Didn't anyone go out to verify the claim?"

"I'm not even sure, but whatever they did, it cost big. Bobby, the idiot who convinced me to lie for him, swore up and down that he'd pay every penny back."

"Which I'm assuming he didn't do?"

"Got that right. I wasn't about to let my folks eat the cost. That was a big part of why I went into the air force. Although it ended up being good for a lot more than that."

A couple approached, and while Seth pulled her closer to the building, he nodded, and the guy nodded back. Once they were alone again, Hannah stepped in a little closer so their hands brushed, not just their shoulders. "It sounds like you got the short end of the stick from the moment you got in that car."

Seth grunted. "I didn't know then that Bobby wasn't just a passing college alcohol abuser. He blamed me for him being a drunk."

"Uh…"

"He's been in and out of rehab for seven years. And according to him, because I'd covered for him, he hadn't been able to hit bottom. So I'm responsible for him failing for the rest of his life."

"Tell me you aren't still friends with that ass."

"Nope. I severed all ties as soon as I wised up."

She finally gave in and threaded her fingers through his, giving his hand a squeeze. "I'm sorry you had to go through that. I may not have known you for long, but I'm absolutely certain you didn't deserve that run of rotten luck."

He slowed. Gave her a smile that almost reached his eyes. "The worst of it was the ripples, you know? Jasper never missed an opportunity to run me down. In fact, he took a great deal of pleasure trashing the entire Landers family—past, present and future. For way too long I kept up the pretense, lying for Bobby, foolishly mistaking stupidity for honor. I still can't believe I chose that jerk's scholarship above my family. Jesus. I don't know if I'll ever forgive myself for that."

"Tell me something," she said, her chest aching with what he'd been through. "If this had all happened to Nathan or Clint, would you have forgiven him?"

Seth tensed. Even his hand tightened around hers to the point of almost being painful. She'd clearly asked the wrong question, although she couldn't believe Seth was the kind of man who would hold a mistake over his brother's head.

Instead of letting it go, which would have been the easy thing, she held on tighter. "What happened? What am I missing?"

The way he looked at her, it was as if he wasn't sure what to make of her or her nosiness, but dammit, she wanted him to let this thing out. She would be leaving soon, and whatever he told her, his secret would leave with her.

"Look, it's all in the past. My folks know what happened, I fessed up to everything, and I've been working hard to do my fair share, so—"

"I'm sure that's all true. But...?"

For a long second she thought he might tell her to mind her own business, but then his shoulders relaxed, his eyes stopped being so wary.

"Did I tell you I spent the weekend in jail?"

She nodded.

He struggled for a second, and just when she thought he was going to let it all out, he shut down. Not completely. But she could see there was something he wasn't going to say, and she'd done enough pushing.

"Well, that sucked," he said.

"I imagine so."

Just before they reached her rental car, he pulled her into a long, heated kiss. As far as distractions went, it worked pretty well.

"See you at the motel?" he said.

She nodded, her chest still tight, despite the kiss, as she watched him head back in the direction they'd come from.

Half a car length away he stopped. "By the way, why were you taking notes?"

A shadow obscured most of his face. If he'd wanted to hide his expression, he couldn't have planned it better.

"Habit," she said easily. "A symptom of my job. You'd think I could turn it off for a week, wouldn't you?"

She could see a little of his smile. What she couldn't tell was whether curiosity or suspicion had prompted the question.

HANNAH COULDN'T HAVE felt more relieved to see a smile on Seth's face as he waited for her near the motel's entrance. They'd only been apart for five minutes, but that was plenty of time for him to decide he didn't believe her explanation for taking notes. But there was no point in telling him when she had no idea if anything would come of it.

He was holding a small duffel bag in his left hand and gestured with his right. "After you," he said.

Unable to resist, she brushed against him, and got a quiet grunt as she stepped into the motel lobby. "This is so—"

"Small?" Seth said, as the door slid shut behind them. "Charming."

He raised his eyebrows, and she wished they were in the room already. Both of them naked. And her with the certainty she hadn't given him cause for alarm. She really had to shake the guilt. By asking questions and taking notes, she hadn't harmed him or anyone else. But she had lied to him, and that bothered her.

On the short ride over she'd decided she would not, under any circumstances, think about Jasper, grazing permits or her family. So she dropped the small lie in the same mental box with the other *don'ts* and locked it tight.

"Come on. This beats the heck out of having to be quiet," she said, determined to enjoy the night ahead. "Or getting bug bites on the behind."

"Did you?"

She shrugged. "Might have."

Seth's laugh eased the last of the tension in her shoulders. Didn't make her less nervous about tonight's main event, though. She really wanted them to mesh between the sheets the way they did in every other respect. Somehow, the day they'd gone skinny-dipping didn't really count for her. And not just because it had been a quickie, although having a whole, uninterrupted night would be far more revealing.

Since they didn't have to stop at the front desk, she checked out the small lobby area, which consisted of a pair of burgundy club chairs and a brown loveseat with a coffee table between them. A beige lamp and flared magazines sat on the table. Against the wall behind the chairs was a console table, with a matching lamp and a stack of brochures.

Seth guided her toward the elevator, his big hand splayed across her lower back. "They have a continental breakfast down here from seven to nine. Coffee, muffins and cinnamon buns."

"I doubt we'll be up." She hit the button for the top floor. As soon as the doors closed she pressed up against him. "I mean we'll be wrecked after having sex all night long. Right?"

He lifted one dark brow at her, amusement making his face come alive. Any lingering ghosts from the past had disappeared.

"Hey, I'm not the one with the pocket full of condoms," she said.

"When you're right, you're right." He took her mouth in a very promising kiss, which came to an undignified halt when the elevator lurched to a stop.

Of course their room was at the end of the corridor. By the halfway point, they were speed walking. He used the key card, the door swung open, and there it was. A king bed with four pillows, a comforter and a lime-green quilt folded at the foot. "This room is perfect."

"The only thing you've seen is the bed."

"Is there a bathroom?"

He did something behind her, but she was preoccupied with testing the bounce of the mattress.

"Yep. Shower-tub combo. Sink. Mirror."

"Then I'm good."

He dropped her bag and his own duffel on the floor and picked her straight up into his arms so their eyes met. "This is the best possible end to whatever the hell today was."

"It is, isn't it?"

"There are only a couple of things I can think of that would make it better."

"What, pray tell, would those be?"

"Well," he said, taking a quick nibble at the curve of her jaw. "Removing your clothes, for starters."

"I think we can handle that. Although, you'd have to put me down."

"Really? I like having you like this."

She kind of liked it, too. Framing his face with her hands, she kissed him soundly.

The second she pulled back to catch her breath he loosened his hold so she slid down his body. "I can't decide whether I want to strip you or watch you strip for me."

After rubbing against that solid chest of his both choices sounded exciting. "Rock-paper-scissors?" She held up her fist, ready to play. "Winner chooses?"

Grinning, he brought his own fist up. "I'm pretty good at this," he warned.

"I'm pretty good at what happens after."

He opened his mouth. Nothing came out. He lowered his hand and dropped his chin. "You win. I'll agree to anything you say."

"Ooh. The possibilities are endless," she said, although she'd made up her mind before the game had even begun.

"Remember this," Seth said. "Once I have you naked, I intend to take my time. I've been thinking about this for too damn long. And, for the record, I couldn't care less if someone complains about the noise."

A yummy shiver ran down her spine. "I'm going to strip." She cleared her throat, her mouth gone dry from the way he looked at her. "I want you to strip—"

He had his shirt halfway unbuttoned before she'd finished the sentence.

"What happened to taking your time?"

"Yeah, yeah. Time. Patience. Too many clothes." He yanked his shirt out of his jeans, then motioned for her to hurry up.

Who was she to argue? She whipped off her cocoa-colored top, struggled with her stupid belt and finally managed to unzip her capris, but he was way ahead of her. In fact, he'd taken off almost every stitch—including his boots—all but his dark blue boxer-briefs.

"Oh, jeez." After wiggling her way out of her capris, she still wore her matching leopard-print bra and panties, leaving her to tease him with the final unveiling.

"You," he said, taking a step toward her, "are gorgeous."

She smiled as coquettishly as she knew how, but that felt awkward, so she just reached behind her back and undid her bra without letting it fall. Then she turned around, giving her butt a little wiggle. She felt like a dope and almost started laughing. But no, she would see this through.

Looking over her shoulder, she pushed off one strap, then the other. And in what she hoped was a sexy move, she held her bra out to the side and after a couple of beats, let it fall.

"Well, damn," he said, the words all gravel and need. When she turned around it was clear he'd been…*inspired*…by her performance, even though she wasn't finished.

Closing the distance between them, he whispered, "Let me take it from here."

"Uh-huh."

Seth's nostrils flared, which was way sexier than she ever could've imagined. The hunger in his gaze was so primal it made her tremble.

"Finally," he murmured, in a low rasp that stroked her skin. His fingers threaded through her hair as he eased her into a kiss that had her head spinning.

Touching her both tenderly and with restrained strength, he teased the seam of her lips with his breath and tongue, then let her take a breath only to kiss her again at the exact right moment.

Hannah wanted to climb into his arms and never leave.

She moaned, only realizing after that she'd been moaning all along. They more than fit, right down to their toes.

"Lie down with me," he said, running both hands down her back until he snagged her panties. A second later they pooled around her feet.

In her most eloquent move of the night, she flapped a hand at his briefs until he finally stripped them down. She caught herself staring at his erection, then she yanked the covers to the bottom of the bed and knelt on the edge of the mattress. Seth joined her, and they inched their way to the center of the bed.

Before she could lie down, he wrapped her in his arms, pulled her flush against him. Still on their knees, their height difference had changed, although he was still taller. Broader. And, God, he was hard.

His erection pressed against her, several inches above her V, and was getting her all revved up. She tried to slip her hand between them, but it took a moment for him to give her the room she needed.

She curled her hand around his cock, and he inhaled sharply. "Jesus, woman."

Hannah smiled. "You aren't complaining, are you?"

One more firm stroke and his hand closed around her wrist. "Better stop now," he said.

"What, you forgot your condoms?"

He winced. "Shit."

She felt a moment's panic. "They're still in your pocket, right?"

"Yes. Which is good, or else I'd be running out stark naked to buy more."

"Actually, I'd kind of like to see that," Hannah said, laughing.

He swiped his tongue across her collarbone and down

her left breast, then licked her nipple before catching it gently between his teeth.

Her laughter ended in a whimper.

"Hmm," he murmured, sucking lightly at first. Then harder.

Her hand hadn't migrated too far. But just as her fingers grazed his erection, he moved back and stood. *Spoilsport*, she thought, smiling to herself. At least when he turned to get the condoms, she had the pleasure of staring at his butt.

Must be all that horseback riding. She could, quite literally, stare at him for hours.

He was back quickly, but she was already lying on her side, her head on one of the fluffy pillows. Thinking about how she'd love to trace her tongue over every inch of muscle, each swell and every ridge. She couldn't decide where she'd start, but she damn well knew where she'd end up.

"What's that smile for?" he asked, stretching out beside her, the warmth from his body washing over her, soothing her and turning her on at the same time. He made sure they were able to look straight into each other's eyes, a quirk of his that she liked very much.

"Why wouldn't I be smiling? We're finally—" She paused, wanting to be careful about her wording. "We have privacy and each other. What more could we want?"

Seth's laugh tugged at her heart. He knew, without her saying anything, that she was concerned about jinxing them. Being with him was so easy. Maybe it was a common thread of the vacation sex experience, the thing that made it so appealing, but she had no way of knowing.

"It feels as if it's been more than three days," he said, caressing her arm lightly, then making a smooth move to her breast. He rubbed his thumb over her already beaded nipple, the pleasant friction making her quiver.

"I know," she said. "I'm glad we decided to do this. We should've checked in Sunday night."

"Believe me, I thought about it."

"What stopped you from suggesting it?" she asked, running one finger up the length of his cock.

Jerking, he sucked in a breath. "Oh, so you want to cut to the chase, huh?"

"The chase began the minute we pulled over to look at the stars."

"Yeah," he said, leaning in until his lips were oh, so close. "I suppose it's about time I caught you."

He pulled her up tight, then slipped his hand between her thighs. Finding her already swelling clit, he rubbed it just hard enough. Excited, she accidentally bit his lower lip.

He grunted, but didn't pause.

She touched him everywhere she could reach. His back, his shoulders, loving the way his muscles flexed. The world she knew in Dallas was full of cowboy wannabes and gym rats, and she hadn't given that much thought until Seth.

It made her wonder if things would've been different had they met in Dallas. Would they have hit it off so quickly? Made such a strong connection? The way he turned her on and made her crave him…would it have scared the hell out of her, or made her start thinking about the future?

His breathing had become more rapid, his tongue more insistent. When she realized he'd already put on the condom, she didn't want to wait.

Shoving him to his back, she straddled him, kissing

her plan into his lips. He understood her and reached between them to line himself up.

When she sank down on him they both moaned. His eyes closed briefly, as he thrust up.

He felt wonderful inside her; filling her with warmth; she almost didn't want to move. For one stupid moment she felt cheated that there were so few days left, but then he stole her breath by spinning her onto her back.

Seconds later, he was between her thighs, thrusting in once more. This time, his eyes stayed open.

So did hers.

He didn't look away when he rocked gently forward, kissing her on the lips and giving her hard, aching nipples a light squeeze.

His gaze remained steady, even when he lifted her right leg over his shoulder, hurrying the pace, stroking deeper and faster as she raked her fingernails down his chest.

She was the first to blink when his thumb found her clit once again. Relentless, he rubbed and teased until she felt her climax begin. As it blossomed, she squeezed her internal muscles, making them both moan.

When it hit full force, she spasmed hard. Prickly heat surged through her body. Familiar waves of sensation washed over her, satisfying the ache in her breasts. The emotionally charged pounding in her heart was different.

On her second big pulse he cried out, stretched his neck and froze. His gaze touched her lips, then met her eyes.

"Hannah," he whispered.

The raw, husky sound of her name on his lips stole what scant breath she had left. She couldn't speak.

Seth's hard, muscular body trembled with his release. The moment was utterly silent. Completely perfect.

It took Hannah a while to summon the strength, but when she did, she reached up and swept back the lock of hair that had fallen onto his damp forehead.

His mouth curved in a lazy, exhausted smile. It seemed they were both having trouble keeping their heavy lids up as he collapsed beside her.

The next time she opened her eyes, there was a sheet and blanket covering both of them. Her leg was over his thigh and her head nestled against the dip of his shoulder.

She sighed, feeling utterly safe and happy as she slipped back into sleep.

13

SETH SHOULD'VE BEEN dead to the world after the last few days. He couldn't remember falling asleep, much less how much time had passed, but he'd be willing to bet he hadn't slept for more than a couple of hours. And yet he felt pretty damn energetic and raring to go. Although he wasn't as sure about waking Hannah.

She was beautiful, with her hair wildly splayed across the pillow, her lips slightly parted. He brushed wisps of hair from her cheek, then skimmed his fingers down to her neck, her chest, her gorgeous breasts.

It was a damn shame she lived so far away. Being with her was so easy. He didn't have to plot and plan, try to think what she'd like, or decipher her words and actions to figure out what she *really* meant. She hadn't complained about the last-minute emergencies, silly and avoidable or otherwise. Running a ranch was a 24/7 job. Even some of the local women who knew better got sulky over having a date interrupted.

He couldn't discount the fact that this was temporary. Vacation sex was probably always fast and furious, less complicated. But it wasn't just the sex that made him think of her so often.

She made a sound, high and sweet, and stretched her arm out as she opened her eyes. "I'm so glad you're here," she said with a sleepy smile.

"Me, too."

"Is it the middle of the night?"

"Close to one."

"Sounds like a great time to have more sex."

"My thoughts exactly."

"Okay, you get ready while I go check out the bathroom."

She kissed him quickly on the lips, then hopped out of bed, and he watched her until she closed the door.

Wasting no time, he got another condom ready, although he didn't put it on. He didn't plan on using it right away. In fact, as soon as she came out of the bathroom, he got up to use it, as well.

Hannah was looking impatient by the time he returned, though he couldn't have been gone more than three minutes.

"Don't give me that look," he said, aware her gaze had just lowered. "Do you know how long I waited for you to wake up? Do you have any idea how much restraint—" Her eyes had widened and focused on his face. "What?"

"Why the hell would you do that?"

"Do what?" he asked, sliding in beside her.

"Let me sleep. We can't afford to waste any time."

Seth chuckled, then got that she wasn't kidding. She'd started kissing him before he even hit the pillow. Evidently all was forgiven. And time really was of the essence.

"I knew you went in there to brush your teeth," she murmured, tasting quite minty herself.

He smiled, then slithered his way down her body.

"Wait," she said. "Where are you going?"

In answer, he paused to taste her sweet, hard nipples.

With a soft whimper she started kneading his shoulders. So he stayed to suck a nipple into his mouth and pluck the other one with his fingers.

A minute later, lured by the musky scent of her arousal, he resumed his quest, moving farther down, licking and tasting, until he was perfectly situated between her thighs.

His lips grazed the neatly trimmed patch of hair that guided his mouth directly where he wanted to go. There was no way to stop his moan once he'd spread her lips and finally tasted her.

It didn't take long to have her bucking like a bronc as he brought her to her peak. He had to move fast to save his neck, but that was fine because he couldn't wait another second to be inside her.

This time wasn't so slow and tender, but he wasn't exactly in a rush.

"You shouldn't have put the condom on so fast," she murmured, her voice a breathy rasp. "I wanted to…" she struggled for a breath "…do things."

Seth touched her flushed face. "It's early yet. We can do whatever you want."

She smiled so pretty it made him ache.

SETH OPENED ONE EYE. A narrow stream of sunlight breached the closed drapes and hit him in the face. He turned his head and saw that Hannah wasn't there.

Her side of the bed wasn't even warm.

He stretched out his arms and everything else he could, feeling pleasantly used, like after a really great ride through the foothills.

Oddly, the door to the bathroom was open, and he didn't hear the shower or anything. When he noticed it was 8:40, he figured she'd most likely gone down to the lobby for coffee. He squinted at the piece of paper next to the bedside clock. He rolled out of bed, stretched his back, then picked up the small motel stationery tablet on his way to the bathroom.

I'm getting coffee. Don't go anywhere.

"Where would I go?" he asked, hurrying so he'd be ready when Hannah returned with the coffee—and rolls or muffins. Guaranteed she'd bring some sort of pastry. Although he was hungry enough to want a real breakfast. Bacon, eggs, hash browns, toast, more coffee. Oh, yeah. He'd convince her to his way of thinking. Given their activity level last night, she had to be starving, too.

He decided to take a quick shower, briefly considered squeezing in a shave if he could, but that was probably pushing it. After drying himself off, he walked back into the bedroom with the towel wrapped around his waist, but she still wasn't there.

Huh.

Okay, so she was probably chatting with whoever was manning the reception desk. God, he hoped she wasn't being held hostage by one of the locals, although it was doubtful anyone from town would be hanging out in the motel lobby, especially at this hour.

He put on a pair of boxer-briefs and a new pair of dark blue jeans that really needed breaking in, even though he'd already washed them twice. Sitting on the edge of the bed, he put on socks, eyed his boots and hesitated. It was possible he could talk her into crawling back into bed with him. A muffin would hold them over until they got to the diner for a real breakfast.

His mind wandered back to the night before. He remembered everything, from the way she smelled like unadulterated female, to how she tasted like the ocean on a rainy day.

The last thing he wanted to do was get all worked up only to have Hannah walk in ready to head out for the day, but damn, just thinking about her was already setting his gears in motion.

Stupid, though. Especially when he realized the continental breakfast was over and she hadn't returned.

He didn't waste much time pulling on a shirt and his boots. His teeth were brushed, but he still had day-old scruff darkening his jaw, which he wouldn't worry about now. He ran a hand through his hair, promising himself he'd get a much-needed haircut soon.

Some guy was already in the elevator before Seth caught the door. He looked like a salesman passing through, his suit as well worn as his weathered face. Eventually, they reached the lobby level, and Seth went on the hunt.

He didn't need to go far.

Hannah was sitting in one of the burgundy chairs, leaning toward Sherwood, the BLM rep, who was sitting in the matching chair. They were talking, and it looked as though they'd been at it awhile. Hannah was holding a foam cup with most of her coffee gone.

What could she possibly have to say to him? Did she still have questions after last night's meeting? From where Seth stood, it sure as hell appeared as though Sherwood was happy to tell her anything she wanted to know.

Last night he'd looked pretty damn slick, standing there in front of a room full of ranchers, using PowerPoint to show them all his charts and graphs. But he'd swiftly ditched the props when it was obvious they served to magnify the gap between him and his audience. At least he'd been smart enough to wear jeans and a casual Western shirt, giving the appearance he was one of them.

Today he looked more at ease in gray slacks and a navy blazer over a crisp white Oxford shirt. His light hair was short, neat and combed, with a part that was a little too straight. Seth wouldn't be surprised if the BLM was just a stepping stone on this guy's way to a political career.

Hannah's laughter made Seth's chest clench. He walked over to the cozy couple, making sure his smile was relaxed. But watching Sherwood hand over a business card to her nearly blew Seth's facade.

"Call me any time," Sherwood said with his megawatt smile.

A second later, Hannah looked up. "Seth." He didn't miss her slight jump. "Oh, my God, I'm so sorry. I didn't realize how long I'd been down here." She lifted a lidded foam cup and a cinnamon bun on a napkin that had been sitting on the table. "The coffee's probably cold by now, but I think they're making a fresh pot."

She sounded genuinely sorry, which made him feel like a heel for being so suspicious. Knowing her, she was probably just doing business. He had no doubt she was a hell of a headhunter, and why not try to recruit a guy like slick?

Sherwood had stood immediately, waiting easily for Seth to acknowledge him, and when he did, the man put out his hand. "Morning," he said, shaking firmly. "Hannah and I were just talking about the meeting last night."

"Oh, yeah?"

"I think it went well, all things considered."

"Boy, do we have a different definition of *well*."

Sherwood laughed. "Anytime the topic of property

rights is brought up, whether pertinent or not, tempers soar. But no blood was shed, so I think we did all right."

Seth had to smile at that. The guy had a point.

Hannah's low groan caught Seth's attention. He turned just as Jasper entered the lobby, making a face like he'd just swallowed sour milk. The old guy's clothes looked as though he'd slept in them. Dry mud chipped off his boots with each step, sending up puffs of dust and leaving a trail on the tan carpet.

"Well, don't this make quite the picture," Jasper said, eyeing Sherwood up and down and then glaring at Hannah. "I didn't believe Avery, so I had to come see for myself."

"See what?" Seth asked, moving so he stood directly between the old man and Hannah. "Some people having coffee?"

"That's what you want me to think. Gotta say I'm surprised at you, boy. Cozying up to the government like a common—"

"Oh, my God." Hannah got to her feet, forcing Seth aside. Her face was flushed, her eyes livid. "Are you talking about last night at the Full Moon? What I said to Avery?"

"Don't bother." Seth put a hand on her back. "Trust me on this."

"I was being sarcastic," she said, meeting Jasper's glare. "Trying to show Avery how ridiculous he sounded asking me if I was a government spy."

Sherwood's brows shot up and he laughed.

That only riled Jasper further. Before he responded, Sadie rushed through the door, out of breath, as if she'd been trying to catch up with Parsons.

Seth rubbed the back of his increasingly tense neck. Great. This was turning into a real circus.

"Mr. Sherwood, I apologize. Please don't listen to this jackass," Sadie barely huffed out. "Hannah, you too."

That would be a miracle, Seth thought, as he felt her body go rigid beside him.

"You don't speak for me, *Madam Mayor,*" Jasper said, in a mocking tone. "Hell, you don't speak for anybody. This town never had a more useless person in office."

"Don't worry about it, Mayor," Sherwood assured her with a smile. "I certainly am not." He turned to Hannah. "I must get on the road for another appointment, but it was nice meeting you."

She made a point to smile big. "Nice meeting you, too. Safe travels."

"Thank you," he said, then he picked up his briefcase and a leather overnight bag, nodded at Seth and left.

Jasper glared at the man's back. "That's right, mister government man, go. We don't want your kind around here."

"Oh, shut your damn mouth, Parsons." Sadie looked pissed, her face red enough to be of concern.

"And take your goddamn permits with you," Jasper shouted, though the door had slid closed and Sherwood couldn't hear him.

Patty, who Seth vaguely knew from years ago, stood behind the front desk, watching with an expression of shock.

An older couple, who'd come out of the elevator, gave Jasper a wide berth on their way out of the building.

Seth turned his back on the old man, and smiled at Hannah. "Why don't we go get some breakfast?"

"Sure." Her hands shook slightly as she picked up the coffee and food she'd left on the table.

"I'll get rid of that," Seth said, holding out his hand. He figured it was taking every bit of her willpower not to go after Jasper. Knowing Hannah, she thought this was her fault. She didn't understand that Jasper didn't need an excuse to be an ass.

With a grateful smile, she handed him the cinnamon bun and some crumpled napkins. She blinked. "Oh, wait." She snatched back a napkin that had writing on it. "Thanks," she murmured, glancing around the lobby, then dropping her cup and muffin into a wastebasket.

Sadie and Jasper were going at it, and Seth couldn't see leaving her here with the bastard. "Excuse me, Mayor?" Seth waited for her to look at him. "Would you like to join us?"

"What?" At least her face wasn't so flushed anymore. "Oh, no." She shook her head. "But thanks."

Seth hesitated when it seemed Jasper wasn't going anywhere.

Patty had every right to call the sheriff's office and have him removed from the premises. But it didn't look as though she planned on doing anything but stare.

"I don't know what to make of you, boy." Clearly, Jasper was speaking to him. "I surely don't."

Seth had just taken Hannah's hand, intent on heading for the elevator. And he couldn't decide if he wanted to acknowledge the stupid bastard. If it meant he'd leave, then Seth would play along, but he doubted it.

"I thought you'd learned your lesson. I truly did. But you're just bound and determined to shame your family right into the dirt. Turn the Landers good name into mud."

Hannah and Seth both stopped in their tracks.

Inhaling a slow deep breath, Seth started to count, giving the red dots clouding his vision time to clear.

Not Hannah, though. She spun around to face Jasper,

her tension practically bouncing off the walls. She looked as though she wanted to tear the man apart.

In a weird way, her reaction helped Seth find his calm.

He tugged on her hand. "This is between Parsons and me," he said in a low steady voice.

"But this is all my—"

"Hannah."

She bit her lip, her eyes watering as they met his gaze. She looked down, gave him a small nod and let her hand fall limply to her side.

Sadie had gotten directly in Jasper's face and was trying to force him backward to the door. Not a bad thing, since Seth realized he needed more time to calm down. The bastard had the goddamn nerve to bring up his family? He didn't give a shit that the man was over thirty years his senior. Seth wanted to plaster him to the goddamn cement.

Sadie managed to get him to the exit, then glanced toward the front desk. "Patty, do me a favor, call Grace."

Jasper laughed. "You let your womenfolk do your fighting for you, boy?" Jasper, the prick, was enjoying himself, trying to dodge Sadie, angling right and left to see past her.

Seth hadn't known what he would actually do if he got within striking distance. A part of him wanted to think that he wouldn't have used violence. But he sure as hell hadn't expected to start laughing.

14

HANNAH FELT SICK. She pressed a hand to her stomach, hoping the elevator ride didn't finish her off. "What just happened?"

Seth still had a weird smile on his face and he hadn't quite stopped laughing as he shook his head. "That dumb ass was eating up the attention. I didn't want to really hit him, but if I had, I would've been the one locked up. Probably exactly what he was hoping for." He paused. "Nah, I did want to hit him. I'd still like to punch him. Dumb bastard."

The elevator came to an abrupt halt. Her stomach did a flip.

"You okay?"

"Um, not really." She let him take her hand and usher her out of the elevator. "If I were to hit him, would they lock me up?"

Seth smiled at her. "You're not going to hit anyone. But thanks for wanting to stick up for me."

"Well, who's Grace? Does she get to punch him?"

"He pisses her off enough, I'm sure she'll find a way." He got out the key card. "Grace is the sheriff."

"Oh." Hannah hadn't expected that, but now a couple of things made sense. "That's why you laughed."

"Actually that's when I realized he was trying to goad me into doing something foolish. *My womenfolk,*" he muttered.

They got to their door and he unlocked it. "I did something I probably shouldn't have…" she began as she entered the room. She turned to watch his expression. "I extended our stay for another night."

Seth's face lit up and he put his arms around her. "I planned on doing the same thing."

"Really?"

"Yes, really."

"Even now?"

"What do you mean?" he asked, staring down at her. "You don't still think what happened was your fault."

Hannah wasn't thrilled about him studying her so closely. Lowering her lashes made it easier to break away. In her heart, she knew she did share some of the blame. He didn't understand because he didn't know everything.

"Listen to me," he said, touching her chin gently, raising her face until he could see into her eyes. "Jasper and Avery are part of the package in this town. They're miserable, greedy and vindictive old men. Nothing you did caused Jasper to be that way. He was a bastard long before you got here."

She had to smile at that, even though she knew Seth was just being nice. And then she remembered his laughter. Maybe she hadn't been at the heart of the problem. But she'd been part of it, no matter the history of the town curmudgeons.

Looking up into Seth's kind face, she wanted to kiss him. No, she wanted to lose herself in his kisses, and that was different. Tempting. Instead, she thought about telling him everything. Just putting it all out there about her father, the poor state of the ranch, her idea to help...

"You okay?"

She nodded, grateful when he pulled her close so she could rest her head on his strong, safe chest.

The thing was, it had been a real stroke of luck that she'd run into Sherwood this morning. He'd brought up a few concerns about her plan. It truly was a complicated matter, crossing state lines with livestock, and for all she knew, her next foray into the law and the practicalities might scotch the whole deal.

The last thing she wanted to do was make Seth's life more complicated if she didn't have to. Not that she thought he'd be angry. He'd said straight out he didn't care about the grazing permits. But he cared a whole lot about causing his family grief. And Jasper was the catalyst that could blow up everything.

So maybe she was splitting hairs, but she'd rather wait and make sure of her position before she filled Seth in.

Instead, she ran her hands up to the back of his neck and buried her fingers in his hair. For a second she simply soaked up his warmth as the connection between them sizzled. Nothing like that had ever happened to her before, and she wanted to memorize every second of it.

By the time they did kiss, she'd let all thoughts of Jasper and blame float away. She could still taste the hint of peppermint on Seth's tongue, and when he moved just so, his stubble scratched the side of her cheek. But she didn't mind.

As she rubbed his chin with the pad of her thumb, his stomach rumbled so loudly they both started laughing.

"So, I really should have hurried with that cinnamon roll, huh?"

"To be honest," he said, rocking them both gently from

side to side, "I'm hungry as a bear. I was thinking we could go to the diner. And after we eat, I thought I'd finally take you for that tour of the ranch I've been promising."

"Really? I'd love to…"

"What?"

"Nothing." She grabbed her purse from the bedside drawer and slipped the napkin with her notes and Sherwood's business card inside. "Now that we don't have to pack, let's go eat."

HANNAH HAD ONLY suggested they stop by Abe's Variety store for lip balm because she was finally certain that Seth wasn't still stewing over Jasper or Avery or anything to do with grazing permits. No one who was worried could have put away that much food so quickly.

"You know, we can stop by the Cake Whisperer and pick you up something," he said, as they walked down the packaged goods aisle.

"I'm fine."

"On that tiny breakfast you had?"

The way she'd felt, she was lucky the dry toast had stayed down. At least now her tummy had settled. "Oh, my God," she said, spotting a familiar tin. "These are Walnettos. I haven't had these since my aunt died fifteen years ago. And look! Allsorts! I hated these when I was a kid."

"Glad to see they've cheered you up."

She was happy to be focused on something other than grazing permits. "My tastes have matured," she said, stashing the bag in her basket, along with the Walnettos tin. "Oh, wait, I want to check out the kitchen gadgets."

His grin made her feel the most at ease she'd felt since

the ugly scene this morning. It seemed Seth had a gift for doing that.

"Gadgets, huh? Is that the technical term?"

"No, you're thinking of doodads. Or thingamajigs. You can look it up."

He surprised her with a kiss on the temple before they went to the next aisle. Even if he did think she was nuts, he didn't seem to care.

She was pretty sure she could have found a store like Abe's Variety in Texas, but most of the fun was being here with Seth, and not to be discounted, being on neutral ground. Recapturing the joy they'd shared that day at the swimming hole, before all the other crap had gotten in the way.

As they ambled closer to the front of the store, she could hear the women who'd gathered by the cash register. Not that she was purposely listening but the group had grown since she and Seth had first arrived and met a pair of twins, elderly women dressed in matching cardigans, introduced as the Lemon sisters. Abe, the owner, had implied they were quite the infamous pair.

They'd looked her over as if she might be carrying the plague, and one of them proceeded to tell Abe that he'd better watch his inventory now that the Sundance visitors liked to come to town so often. With a long-suffering sigh of disgust, her sister contradicted her every word.

Hannah had quickly grabbed a shopping basket not daring to look at Seth for fear she'd burst out laughing. When she'd finally risked a glance, she saw that it hadn't fazed him in the least. Guess he really was used to small town chatter.

A minute later, glancing back, Hannah realized Seth had stopped to look at car wax. So she kept perusing the array of interesting stock, and half-heartedly listened as the ladies up front continued to chat. It sounded as if every single sentence ended in a shocked exclamation point. Even the fact that one of the lights outside the sheriff's office had burned out proved newsworthy.

"Can you hear them?" Seth asked, keeping his voice low as he came up behind her.

She nodded, and they exchanged smiles.

"I told you. That's how it is around here. Drama around every corner, real or not."

"It must be exhausting."

"Yeah. But since there's no movie theater…"

Hannah leaned into him and grinned. "You're adorable."

"Just what every man likes to hear."

After kissing his chin, she got caught up trying to figure out a Gilhoolie jar opener. She'd thought she wanted one, but now wasn't so sure.

Seconds later, Abe joined them, and he and Seth started talking. The proprietor seemed like a nice man. He was in his early sixties with a receding hairline and a ruddy complexion. And, apparently, he'd been sweet on Sadie for years. The fact that Hannah had learned that scrap of extraneous information her very first night in town told her so much, now that she thought about it.

Turning back to a butter churning jar, something interesting occurred to her about Blackfoot Falls. It wasn't that the town was so quaint, but it demonstrated how her own hometown was so utterly lacking. Their only store had been an ugly old warehouse without a single surprise to be found on the dusty, packed shelves. Even as a kid, she'd felt an oppressive sense of ennui. Or maybe that was just her family.

Abe had gone back to the register and Hannah continued her foraging. The bell over the door rang, which stopped the conversation of the Lemon twins and company, but not for long.

"Well, good Lord, Louise, you look like you're ready to burst a pipe," someone said.

"Or lay an ostrich egg," came the high-pitched wavering voice of one of the twins.

"Well, you just wait till you hear what I have to say," Louise said, and paused.

"Oh, for heaven's sake, Louise, don't be so dramatic."

"I'm just trying to catch my breath, you old biddy." After a prolonged silence and a loud sniff, Louise continued, her voice trembling, presumably with excitement. "Any of you heard about what happened over at the motel?"

"Yes, that's old news. Besides, I doubt anyone is surprised that Avery made a fool of himself."

"Ladies," Abe said. "Would you please keep it down?"

"It wasn't Avery," Louise said. "Who told you he was at the motel?"

Taking some comfort in the gossips being unable to get their facts straight, Hannah risked a glance at Seth. Shaking his head, he raised his gaze toward the ceiling.

"Avery was at the meeting last night but he wasn't at the motel."

"Better yet," Abe said, more sharply this time. "Go to the diner and talk all you want. This isn't the place."

The women laughed.

"Anyhow, that's not even the best part," Louise said. "That government man from the BLM was there this morning, and guess who he was getting all kinds of information from?" She paused. "Seth Landers, of all people."

Hannah froze and her stomach clenched so hard she thought she might be sick. Seth closed his eyes. He might have recognized the different voices, but she supposed it didn't matter.

"And that little floozy he's been cozying up to, turns out she's a government spy."

They all gasped.

"You know they're both here right now," said one of the twins, her whisper meant to be sotto voce, but it carried far enough.

"No!" A pronounced silence followed.

"I don't care," someone said, her quieter tone belying her claim. "Doesn't that Landers boy look like butter wouldn't melt in his mouth. What his poor family must be going through."

Why in hell had Hannah said that crap to Avery? She was so used to being flip, it hadn't crossed her mind that there could be ramifications. That it would all crash down on Seth.

"Okay, that's it," he said, although he didn't sound angry. Just tired. "You done?"

She put her basket down where she stood. "Am now."

He held out his arm, and she took it, like they were going to the prom. Seth nodded at the whole group as they passed. Abe couldn't even meet their eyes, but the gossips had no remorse whatsoever. If they did, it was overrun by their curiosity.

As soon as they were outside, Seth said, "Look, don't worry about it. It's nothing I'm not used to."

Which was precisely the problem. He'd told her last night how much pain he'd caused his family, and with her stupid, thoughtless comments, she'd stirred up a huge hornet's nest.

"Can I say something?"

"What's that?"

"What if I were to go back inside and swear to them

that I'm not a government spy and spreading that around just makes them sound like big fat idiots?"

Seth smiled. "I'm not your keeper. You can do whatever you want. But if you're asking me if it would do any good? Not a chance."

They started walking toward the truck.

"I could also tell them that Rachel and I are old friends and she'll vouch for me." She glanced at Seth when he didn't respond, and only then did she realize he was more upset than he'd let on. She doubted he'd even heard her.

"You know the thing that gets me? All that stuff with the DUI happened ten years ago. Back when I was just a stupid college kid. But to the people around here, it might as well have happened last month."

"They can't all be like this," she said.

He shook his head. "They aren't. There are just enough people like them, though, to make it hard. I honestly thought it would have all blown over by now. Guess I should have stayed away awhile longer."

"I doubt your family would agree."

He slowed them down to a stop. "You're right. I'm not going to let some gossips ruin our day. You ready to go see the world famous Whispering Pines ranch?"

She managed a smile, but it slipped the moment she remembered… "How long does it take for gossip to get out to the ranches?"

"Don't worry about it. Unless my mom was shopping or something, this nonsense won't make it out to the ranch for a long time."

15

"ANYTHING IN PARTICULAR you want to see first?" Seth asked, as he parked the truck under a shady tree near the barn.

"The place looks deserted," Hannah said, still feeling a bit nervous about the gossip, his family, her big mouth, pretty much everything. The persistent knot in her tummy hadn't loosened all that much. Probably guilt. "Is it because you're not here cracking the whip?"

"Oh, that's good. We'll ask Clint. He'll like that."

"Gee, thanks. Give him a great first impression of me."

"Hell, everyone's already heard all about you from Murray."

"Even your parents?" She gazed toward the house, knowing his mom had taken a casserole to a sick neighbor and was visiting with the woman for a while.

Taking her hand, Seth's eyes narrowed. "Your hand is ice cold," he said, sandwiching it between his warm palms. "We didn't have to come. In fact, we can turn around right now."

"No, of course not. I want to see everything."

"That could take a few days."

"Well, then I just might have to extend my vacation."

Seth looked startled. "Can you do that?" he asked, hope sparking in his eyes. "Would your boss be okay with it?"

"This is only my second vacation in six years—he'd better not complain." Once again, she'd shot her mouth off without thinking. If, by chance, the deal went through, she'd need the extra days to take care of some business on this end. But now, she'd given Seth the wrong impression, letting him think she'd be staying for him. Which she wanted very much to do if he wasn't too angry with her.

She should've already told him. Each new incident with Jasper, or anything to do with the permits, pushed her into a tighter, darker corner.

She cleared her throat and smiled. "Where do you suggest we start?"

He didn't answer. Just looked at her, his eyes dark and probing, as if he could see all the little lies and omissions she kept rationalizing.

"I'm sorry. I shouldn't have said anything until I figured out if I could afford the time off."

"What's wrong, Hannah?"

"It's not really about my boss. My clients have certain expectations—"

"That's not what I'm talking about," he said. "But you know that."

She swallowed hard. "It's been a rough morning. More for you, I know, but—but can we try to salvage the day and not…" She shrugged, wishing the whole matter could drop that simply.

"I thought that's what I was doing."

"Yes, you're right."

He studied her for an ungodly long moment. "Okay,"

he said finally. "We can get around by horse or ATV, your choice."

"What about the truck?" She saw the confusion in his face, so obviously that was a dumb question. "Or do you mean we'd take one ATV and double up? Because I've never driven one before."

"We could do that, or go on horseback. You'd miss out on a lot if we took the truck."

She sighed. "I love horses. I really do, but I'm not—"

"Hannah, I'm sorry. You told me that first night and I forgot."

"I did go for a short ride with Rachel and some other guests and I didn't embarrass myself, so…" She shrugged. "There's that…"

"Tell me what would make you the most comfortable and that's what we'll do."

"Okay." She took a deep breath. "ATV with me riding in back of you."

"You got it. And, hey, I won't even have to saddle it."

"Make sure there's gas, though."

Seth laughed. "I'll try to remember," he said, leading her into the barn. "Grab a couple bottles of water out of the fridge, would you? Do you have a color preference?"

After spotting the ancient refrigerator at the back, she looked over at him. "What do you mean? The ATV?"

"Yep, which one?"

"Are you making fun of me?"

"No," he said, unable to hold back a laugh.

Hannah took a quick look around. She didn't see anyone but… "Consider yourself flipped off."

Seth really howled at that, and for a few glorious minutes she forgot all about town gossips, Jasper and her dad.

Then her cellphone rang. The call was from home. Had to be her mom—aka The Intermediary. Hannah's dad had never called her once in her entire life. She stared at her cell, not wanting to answer. If only she hadn't jumped the gun and told them about her grand plan to save the day. She'd drop the matter right now. Forget she'd even heard about grazing permits. But if she bowed out now, her dad would see it as another one of her failures and that's why he'd needed a son.

Yeah, because gender made up for everything. Too bad her mom hadn't given him a son who'd grown up like Jasper.

"Hey, I don't mind giving you some privacy." Seth's voice made her jerk.

She'd forgotten he was there. And the fact that her father could make her forget a good man like Seth for even ten seconds was a damn crime.

Smiling her thanks, Hannah shook her head. Depending on how the conversation went she'd just wander outside if she had to. "Hey, Mom."

"It's Dad."

Her stomach dropped to her knees. "Dad?"

"That's what I said."

She cleared her throat, then was hit with another shot of adrenaline. "Is everything okay?"

"We're suffering a goddamn drought. What kind of stupid question is that?"

"I meant with Mom," she mumbled softly. How could she continue to let him make her feel like a cowering ten-year-old?

"She's not home. She's out shopping. That's one of the reasons I'm calling. I don't want you worrying her with ranch business. Your mom doesn't have a head for that kind of stuff. All she does is get nervous and ask stupid questions."

Hannah bit her lip, briefly closed her eyes. She had

the fleeting thought she should defend her mother, who certainly was not too *stupid* to understand that his stubbornness just might force them into bankruptcy. God, he was such an ignorant bully. Well, bullshit on that. "And the other reason?"

At first he responded with silence. Probably hadn't expected her brisk tone. "That thing you talked to her about the other day. You remember?"

Her mouth completely dry, she headed for the fridge. "Of course."

Part of her wanted him to tell her what a stupid idea it was and he didn't want to hear anything more about it. That would certainly solve her problem here. In fact, she should just swallow her pride, beat him to it. Tell him it wasn't feasible after all, and stop trying to wring a drop of emotion out of him.

"Can you explain more about that?" he asked, his usual gruffness toned down half a notch.

Hannah nearly dropped the phone. She glanced at Seth, or at least at the spot where he'd been standing moments ago. Turning around she saw him stop just outside the barn, far enough that he couldn't overhear her conversation.

Her heart nearly snapped in two. If she caused him any more pain it would kill her.

"This is what I know so far..." The other part of her had begun speaking before she knew it, the part of her that was a foolish little girl who still yearned for her dad's approval.

And as she continued, Hannah turned her back to Seth. Because she couldn't bear to look at him, knowing everything she'd been hiding.

Two HOURS LATER, Seth still couldn't shake the image of Hannah talking to her father, her shoulders slumped, her eyes dull and lowered. She'd looked so…fragile. It was the damnedest thing; even her voice had changed. The spunkiness was gone.

He'd given her a baseball cap to keep the sun off her face as they rode together on the ATV. The way she hung on to him, her arms wrapped snugly around his waist the way a passenger would ride a motorcycle, made him smile. He wondered if she knew she didn't have to hold on so tight, or even hold on at all. He liked it, though, especially when her breath and lips tickled his ear, so he didn't say anything.

"What are they doing?" she asked, letting go briefly to point at Heath chucking blocks of salt out the back of the old pickup Joe was driving.

Seth slowed the ATV so it wouldn't be so noisy. Across the large pasture, Heath looked over and waved a hand.

"They're putting out salt licks. Cows need salt and minerals, just like we do."

"Those blocks look heavy."

"Fifty pounds each." Seth watched the men as they returned to work. They were spreading them too far apart. The licks would kill the grass. "Hey, you mind if we—"

"Of course not. Whatever you need to do."

He let the engine idle and turned his head to look at her, see if the cap and sunblock were protecting her skin. Her nose was still pink, but that was from before.

"What?" Slapping a hand on the slightly oversized cap, she tipped her head back so she could see him from under the brim. "You better not be counting my freckles."

"I already did the other day. You have eleven of them, right here across the bridge of your nose," he said, tracing the pad of his thumb over the faint dots, and then smiling at her indignant expression. "By the way, the land we're on now? This is part of the acreage that we bought four months ago. It's greened up nicely. We'll be moving some of the herd over."

She swept a gaze across the pasture to the tree line where some spots were bare. "Hasn't it been green for a while?"

"Not too long. As counterintuitive as it sounds, over-grazed grass always greens up before anything else. That surprises people who don't know better. The old man who owned it quit raising cattle a few years before he died, so all this land remained untouched."

"Who sold it to you? His kids?"

"Yep. They live out of state and only wanted to keep their father's cabin and three acres. They let us have it for a good price."

"I bet that happens a lot, huh? The kids move to cit-ies or bigger towns, then sell off the ranch after their parents die."

"It's fairly common. Around here it's a little different. It doesn't happen as often as you might think."

She nodded absently and got that faraway look in her eyes again. That was twice now, ever since she'd spoken with her dad.

Noticing that Joe was headed toward the creek, Seth decided he'd head them off before they hit the dirt road and started spinning up dust.

He turned the ATV and drove slowly, keeping pace with the ancient pickup.

Hannah automatically slid her arms around him again, bringing back his smile. "Did the purchase have anything to do with you moving back?" she asked. "Did you have to swear a blood oath that you'd stay forever?"

Seth laughed. "Oh, yeah, I had to sign a contract and promise to give up my firstborn child if I reneged."

She went perfectly still, then lightly bit his right shoulder. "I didn't fall for that for a second. Just so you know."

The pickup stopped. Heath stood in the back and motioned to Seth, who'd gotten distracted by Hannah's question and had done a piss-poor job of keeping pace. It looked as though Heath was asking if they should wait, so Seth nodded and picked up some speed.

Seth snorted to himself. Those two jokers wouldn't have bothered stopping to see what he wanted if Hannah hadn't been with him. Undoubtedly they'd heard about her and wanted a look for themselves.

He kept the introductions short, told them where to put the blocks, and after Hannah sipped some of her water, he got the two of them headed toward the calving shed. They hadn't seen Clint yet, and Seth figured he ought to touch base with him. Bad enough Seth was feeling a bit guilty knowing Clint was working his ass off.

But, damn it, Hannah wouldn't be around much longer. Seth was already dreading the day they had to say goodbye. His thoughts returned to her question. He wondered if she was putting out feelers. Trying to figure out how tied he was to the Whispering Pines, to living in Montana. To his family.

Much as it would pain him to tell her, assuming the question ever came up, Dallas—or anywhere else that wasn't right here on Landers land—wasn't in his future.

"Do I hear water?" Hannah asked. "Are we close to the creek? Because I'm not going skinny-dipping today."

Seth grinned. "Are you sure you don't want to? Just to cool off?"

Hannah laughed, and damned if he knew what that meant. Could go either way with her. She hugged him tighter and lifted her chin to the wind hitting their faces. And there went the hat.

He'd been waiting for that to happen.

"Oh, shit. Seth. Wait." She shook his shoulder. "Seth, stop."

He stopped. Before she fell off and hurt herself.

"Just hold on," he said. "I know about the cap. I'm turning around."

She contorted her upper body trying to track the stupid cap. "But it's getting away…"

It didn't matter, but there was no telling her that. "Hannah, just put your arms—oh, Jesus."

She'd jumped off and was running in the wind and tall grass.

Seth cut the engine. He went after her like a shot, and tackled her twenty seconds later.

16

THE DENSE GRASS cushioned them, though he made sure his body broke her fall. And the wind carried off her peals of laughter. Her face was red, and so was her neck and throat. Her skin was warm and soft beneath his palm.

"I—I can't believe you—" Out of breath, still laughing, she struggled to speak. "You—you tackled me."

"I did."

Sprawled across him, she tried to push herself up, her own laughter her biggest obstacle. She finally gave up. "You're squashing me."

"You're on top."

"Oh," she said, and laughed harder.

He rolled over, taking her with him and pinning her to the grass. "Now I'm squashing you."

Hannah laughed until she hiccupped.

And hiccupped.

Her knee almost put him out of commission for the day.

Seth made sure her legs were secure, then braced himself on his elbows, lazily brushing the hair off her flushed cheeks as if he had all the time in the world.

With his head shading her face, she looked up at him, the sunlight turning her eyes the color of cinnamon.

"Hey, I need water," she said, between hiccups and a stray giggle. "Seriously. I drink it while I hold my breath and count to ten."

Her lips were a deep rose and slightly damp. Her pale skin even *looked* soft. He lowered his head and kissed her mouth. She gasped and gave him a light shove, before locking her arms around his neck.

They kept kissing. He'd pull back and she'd lift her head to keep their lips pressed together. And when she needed air and broke it off, he'd give her a few seconds and then they would go at it again.

He had no idea how long they'd been lying there. He hadn't even wondered about it until the sun disappeared. Turned out a cloud was blocking it. They had a while before the sun dropped behind the Rockies.

Hannah sighed. "I wish this afternoon would never end."

"I'd be okay with that," Seth murmured, and inhaled the pleasant minty scent of her hair.

"I think the cap's a goner, though."

He smiled. "I don't know…with this wind it could be waiting for us in the barn."

"Wouldn't that be hysterical?" She laughed, then her eyes went wide. "Hey, my hiccups are gone. You cured them."

"Some guys' kisses can awaken a sleeping princess. I cure hiccups."

"Don't underestimate yourself. Take it from a girl who knows more than she'd like to about hiccups. This is major. Next time I…" She trailed off, blinking, and looking away. "We should go."

"Yeah, we should." He got to his feet and extended

his hand. She clasped it and he pulled her up. "I want you to meet Clint and Lila before they go off to work on the new house."

"Do me a favor?"

"Name it."

"Please don't tell anyone I grew up on a ranch."

He studied her a moment. "No problem. I won't mention it."

"It just makes me look stupid," she said, as they walked to the ATV.

"What do you mean?"

"Because I don't know things that a person who grew up on a ranch should. I wanted to kick myself for telling you that first night."

"For what it's worth, I didn't think much of it." Seth plucked a blade of grass clinging to her hair. "You sounded surprised that your dad called," he said, after promising himself he wouldn't bring it up.

"Surprised? I was shocked. He's never called me before. Ever. I was afraid something had happened to my mom."

"Everything all right?"

Hannah nodded, and seemed awfully interested in her fingernails all of a sudden. "When I was in college my mom would phone and say my dad wanted her to call and see how I was doing. It was a lie. I'm not sure why she felt she needed to do that. I asked her once, but she kept insisting it was my dad's idea."

"Must be a mom thing."

"Yours, too?"

Seth nodded. "Yeah, when I was on the lam." At least he got her to smile.

They climbed back on the ATV and rode around for another hour without finding the cap or Clint. Murray was doing some repairs on the calving shed and told them Paxton was searching for a bull that had wandered off.

"I should've brought a radio with me," Seth muttered, although he hadn't seen the bull and he had phone service. "Have you seen enough for now?"

Hannah wrinkled her pink nose and nodded. "You feel guilty, don't you?"

"A little." He shrugged. "I shouldn't, though. Nobody expected me to come back as an indentured servant."

He took a shortcut back to the barn, sorry that he hadn't thought sooner about Hannah not having the cap to shade her face.

After he parked and they both climbed off, he said, "If you're feeling adventurous later, you could try driving the ATV."

"I'll use my adventure points back at the motel." She grinned up at him. "Unless you'd prefer to teach me about all-terrain vehicles."

"Nope. Your idea has a great deal of merit. Let's roll with that."

"Hey, you trying to avoid me?" It was Clint, walking out of the smaller west barn on the other side of the corrals.

"I wondered where you were hiding." Seth steered them toward him. "Damn, you're filthy."

Clint pulled off his work gloves and used the bandana from his back pocket to mop his sweaty face. "Somebody left me to steam clean the diesel retriever all by myself. But I won't name names," he said, grinning. "You must be Hannah."

"I am, and the reason you got stuck with all the work."

"That's okay. Glad to see my baby brother has good taste."

"Baby brother." Seth snorted. "He says that to annoy me."

"Looks like it's working," Hannah said, shading her eyes and squinting at him.

Clint laughed.

So did Seth. "You know if Mom is home yet?" he asked his brother.

Clint looked past them. "There she is now."

She'd just turned down the quarter-mile driveway in her silver SUV, inching along, as usual.

"I'll catch up with you guys after I clean up," Clint said. "I think Lila's in the house doing wedding stuff."

Obviously his mom had spotted them. Instead of driving around to the garage, she parked in front of the house where they were headed.

"Did you warn her that I was coming?" Hannah asked, starting to tense.

"Warn her? Why? Were you planning to do something scary?"

"Scary?"

"You know. Like karaoke?"

That got him a punch in the shoulder that he'd expected, but it was worth it to see the fire in her eyes. So different from the way she'd looked talking to her father.

Seth didn't know why he hadn't been able to let that go yet. Except that any father who made his child look so deflated like that needed someone to knock some sense into his thick head. Imagine, having an amazing daughter like Hannah and treating her like a disappointment.

He knew a little something about that, but that had only been the one time, and even though the experience still stuck in his craw, there was no doubt in his mind that his father, both his parents, loved him.

As they neared the SUV, Hannah's steps slowed. "Do you think she knows about what happened? Can you tell by her expression?"

"Hannah, honestly. Don't sweat it. She was visiting a sick neighbor. She couldn't have heard anything. And if she did, it's no big deal."

"Well, hello," his mother said, sliding out of the SUV, shading her eyes and smiling at Hannah.

"Hey, Mom," Seth said. "This is Hannah Hastings. I was just showing her the ranch. Hannah, this is my mom, Meryl Landers."

"It's lovely to meet you." She clasped both Hannah's hands and gave her a light squeeze. "I've heard nice things."

"Me, too," Hannah said softly. "About all of you."

"Well, good. I hope that means you two are staying for supper," Meryl said, releasing Hannah. "Seth? Hannah, would you, please?"

Hannah looked at him. "I'd love to," she said, and he supposed if you didn't know her, her hesitation wouldn't have shown.

"Wonderful. I'm going to get started on it right now." Meryl grabbed her purse. "Oh, for heaven's sake. I almost forgot. Would you two mind bringing in the groceries?"

Hannah glared at him.

Seth could only shrug.

THE MINUTE ALL the groceries were put away or set out on the kitchen island, Hannah grabbed Seth by the arm and nearly pulled him off balance, "Excuse us for just a minute, Mrs. Landers?"

"Meryl, please."

"Meryl," Hannah repeated, and walked briskly to the living room.

She dragged him past the couch and chairs, straight into the family room. Only to stop short when they spotted Lila on the telephone, a whole table full of wedding paraphernalia spread out around the floor in front of her like a rug.

"No, no. We'd decided on a choice between the bourbon-glazed salmon and beef tenderloin for the main, and crab cakes for the appetizer." Lila noticed them and gave a rather tired wave to him, a brighter one to Hannah. "Could you hold on for one second, please?" she said, before she put her phone in her lap. Then she grinned at them. "Hannah, right? I hope we can talk later?"

Hannah smiled. "I'd like that."

"Great," Lila said, then waved again as she put on her game face.

Seth was unceremoniously pushed out of the family room and down the hall until she locked them both in the guest bathroom.

Everything about her said fight-or-flight, from the rapid breathing to the dilated pupils. "We have to tell her."

"My mom? She could already know."

"If she already knows, then she'd expect us to tell her."

"What?"

"Seriously, we have to tell her. Although maybe we should wait until after dinner. I don't want to ruin her appetite. That would be terrible. And maybe we should wait until everyone's here. Do Lila and Clint usually eat dinner with you? And what about your father? Oh, God, you think he knows?"

"Hannah—"

"Maybe I should just go. I could say I'm getting a migraine, and that would only be a little fib because I already have a headache. I wanted to meet your parents when everything was nice so they would think I'm nice, and now they're going to see that I'm a sarcastic bitch who doesn't know when to keep her mouth shut."

"Are you going to let me talk?"

She blinked. "Yes, of course. Go ahead."

He took hold of her arms, and Jesus, he could feel her trembling. "Hannah, honey, you're getting all upset for nothing. I told you, none of it was your fault."

"Right. I never said I was a government spy. Out loud."

"Nathan was there. He knew you were being facetious."

Hannah stared at him, her mouth open. She clamped a hand over it. He pried it away and she said, "How could I have forgotten about Nathan? He heard me be an idiot."

"This is ridiculous. My parents wouldn't believe it for a second. No one with half a brain would—"

"That isn't the point. I goaded Avery and Jasper, and that's why they're badmouthing you."

"The minute I said I wanted nothing to do with the whole thing, I lit the fuse. Not you." He kissed the tip of her nose. "Unless there's something you aren't telling me," he whispered, "like you really are a spy." He felt bad teasing her when she trembled again.

She lowered her gaze, the worry lines on her forehead unsettling. "I fanned the flames, though."

"I promise, it'll be okay. We'll wait until everyone's in the kitchen, which should be in about thirty minutes. They know Jasper and Avery, so it won't come as a surprise that they got out of control. Then we'll sit down and have a great meal."

Her eyes closed and he watched her pull herself together. It made him want to kiss her until every bad thing that had ever happened to her was erased from her memory. "Good plan," she said, and opened the bathroom door.

She found the way back to the kitchen without a wrong turn, which was kind of impressive considering how the house was laid out. Seth stayed close behind, hoping she didn't have a meltdown. Maybe he was wrong to ask her to stay. But he really wanted her to meet his family. He couldn't say why it was important to him. It just was.

"What can I do to help?" Hannah asked, sounding normal.

"You can finish cutting up the vegetables for the salad," Meryl said, wiping her hands on her apron as she moved over to check something boiling on the stove. "If there's anything you don't like, just put it in a separate bowl."

"Everything looks great to me." Hannah washed her hands first, then used the big knife and started cutting carrots.

Seth went to the fridge and brought out water and a pitcher of iced tea.

"Smells good in here."

Seth turned. "Hey, Dad, you just get home?"

"Nah, I was in the stables." He smiled at Hannah when she glanced over her shoulder. "Hello."

"That's Hannah," Seth said, winking at her. "This is my dad, Doug."

"We'll have to shake hands later," she said, "but it's lovely to meet you. Boy, there is no question that you're the father of your sons."

That made everyone but Hannah laugh. She just turned pink.

"You're right," Clint said, walking in behind him, fresh from a shower, his hair damp. He went straight for the silverware and loaded up his hands. "We all look like Dad, but thankfully, we have Mom's sweet temperament."

"Now, you just hold on there…" their dad grumbled good-naturedly.

More chuckles. A smile from Hannah. Seth was glad she looked more relaxed.

"Seth, honey, why don't you take care of drinks and salad dressings?"

"I will, Mom, but first there's something you guys need to know. Last night the BLM meeting was about what you'd expect. Jasper Parsons was the pain in the ass we all know and don't love, and Avery Phelps is his new sidekick."

"Drunk, as usual, I'm guessing," Clint said.

"Too true." Seth's gaze was on Hannah. "Anyway, Avery followed us to the Full Moon and started flinging crap around. Everything's a conspiracy, everyone's out to get him."

"So I heard," Meryl said. "That man knows how to make a nuisance of himself better than anyone I've ever met."

"Nah," his dad said. "Jasper wins hands down."

Hannah's head was bowed. The knife had stilled.

"So, this morning, Jasper found us getting coffee. The guy from the BLM happened to be there at the same time. So Jasper got on this kick that I was in cahoots with the government and that Hannah was a government spy—"

"But only because I'd said that the night before. At the bar. To Avery, but I was kidding." Hannah had turned around, her face flushed. "He asked if I was a spy and I said yes, just being a smart aleck. I never meant for it to—"

Clint burst out laughing. "I wish I could've seen that. Avery's eyes must've bugged out of his head."

Seth smiled and hoped his brother's reaction would help ease Hannah's tension. "Obviously Hannah was being facetious. We were with Nathan and Woody, and they knew it. Anybody who overheard wouldn't think otherwise. But then, this morning, after the fiasco with Jasper, we stopped by Abe's. The rumors were already flying. About how I'm letting down my family again. Dragging the Landers name through the mud."

For some reason, Seth's chest tightened. He could feel his gut twisting into a knot. And it finally hit him.

He'd been so busy worrying about Hannah, he hadn't realized he wasn't all that sanguine about having this conversation. He kept his gaze on her, fearing that if he looked at his father he'd see something. A wince, a shake of the head. Or that his mom would look away, even for a second.

Fear gripped him. That he'd disappointed them again. That all his efforts to make things right couldn't quite erase the shame and grief he'd brought down on his family.

And he also knew that if that happened, he'd resent it forever. All because he'd held back and never dealt with the one thing that had hurt the most, the thing that had been eating at him for ten years now.

Guess Hannah wasn't the only one with issues. Well, he wasn't going to stand by like a helpless kid. No matter what he saw when he looked at his folks, he and his dad needed to have a talk.

"Oh, I heard that nonsense in town," his mother said, pouring green beans into the colander in the sink. "And I was only in the market for twenty minutes. You'd think people around here would have enough to do."

The rest of the room was so quiet he could hear the cows lowing from the back pasture.

Hannah was staring at him…or rather through him, and he couldn't quite figure out what she was thinking. And when he finally looked into his father's eyes, he just saw his dad. Not a single feather ruffled.

In fact, he seemed more concerned with what was on the stove. As for his mom, she just smiled at him, and

slapped his dad's hand when he tried to snitch a piece
of chicken.

"Is that it?" Clint asked.

Seth nodded. "That's it."

"Good. 'Cause I'm starving. I'll go get Lila and let's
get this show on the road."

Relieved by his family's reaction, for Hannah's sake,
and for his own as well, he didn't understand why Hannah was swiping a tear from her cheek.

Right before they all sat down, he found a moment to
get her alone in the kitchen. "You okay?"

Tears welled again, and his gut clenched until he
watched a smile lift her lips. "You," she said, her voice
a little stuffed-up, "have the most wonderful family in
the whole world."

"I don't know about that."

She put her hand right over his heart. "I do," she whispered. "I do."

17

THE MOTEL LOBBY was deserted. No one stood behind the front desk, which suited Hannah fine. That left a clear path to the elevator. She didn't have to smile, wave or make small talk. Not that having to do any of those things would've killed her.

She couldn't remember ever being on such an extreme emotional roller coaster over the course of one day. In a way she was lucky, certainly luckier than a lot of women her age. She liked her job, and she was largely successful at it. That made for many days, weeks even, of smooth sailing—no drama or crazy stress. Just as long as she stayed away from her father.

Her social life wasn't too bad. She'd dated different guys here and there, but no one who'd rocked her world. Even that she hadn't sweated. In the back of her mind, she'd always assumed it would happen someday. Generally speaking, her life was good, not great, but pretty damn good.

Spending five days in Montana had completely screwed up everything.

"What are you so busy thinking about?" Seth pushed the button for their floor.

"Tonight. Dinner. You."

"It didn't look like all those thoughts were happy ones."

She smiled at his concern. "Okay, I confess. A thought or two about my dad might've sneaked in."

"Anything you want to get off your chest?"

The elevator door closed just in time.

"The exact opposite," she said, and put his hand on her left breast.

He rubbed her nipple through the layers of her top and bra. She stretched up and he bent his head until their lips met. The amount of electricity generated between them in that fraction of time could've powered the motel.

"Oh, God, I forgot to tell you."

His hand stilled. "What?"

"Tomorrow. We're invited to a barbecue. At the Sundance."

"Oh, Jesus," he said, sounding stricken. "That would mean getting out of bed."

"Right," she said. "We don't have to go."

The elevator stopped. Torn between wanting him to keep using his thumb versus hurrying so they could get naked, she finally gave in to common sense and got moving.

"Something else before I forget…"

"Yes," he said, patiently trailing after her down the corridor.

"I know you feel badly about Clint having so much work, so I think you should go out to the ranch tomorrow and give him a hand."

"Hell, I don't feel that badly."

"Liar," she said over her shoulder. "Besides, I have things to do in the morning."

Seth rubbed his shadowed jaw. "I can tell he's worn out. What with the wedding planning…"

"So, yes, go. While I'm feeling generous. But only because I'm happy I get to sleep with you tonight."

"Just sleep?"

She turned to face him, her back against their door. "What do you think?"

"I'd hate leaving you," he murmured, kissing the side of her neck. "You're going home soon."

"Not tomorrow. Besides, I'll be busy for a few hours. Then we can meet up at the Sundance around six and eat food we don't have to cook. And I'll get to see Rachel. She's been so busy with trail rides and stuff with the guests."

"Ah." He slipped his key card into the lock, then eased her into the room, his eyes holding her captive. "I want you," he said, his voice low and his gaze hungry. "I don't even understand what you do to me."

Those last barely intelligible words thrilled her to her very core.

As he moved in to kiss her, she slipped her hand between them, her palm sliding down past his belt to the hard erection that was already straining. All for her.

His hips jerked forward and his gasp tugged on her lips. "Naked," he said. "Now."

She nodded. "Now is perfect." She yanked off her shirt, tossing it as he unbuttoned his.

"I thought cowboy shirts had snaps."

"Uh, not really my style."

Reaching in back to unhook her bra, she shook her head. "Very short-sighted."

"I can see the error…" he yanked the rest of his shirt out of his jeans "…of my ways. I'll buy a dozen tomorrow."

She threw her bra at the chair, then as she went to unzip her jeans, one of Seth's sleeves got caught on his wrist while he was trying to shake it off. That started a fit of giggles, which hadn't been her plan, but oh, God, he was just so cute.

"I swear to—" He jerked the sleeve free, then tackled his jeans with fierce determination.

She stopped laughing when he stood before her, naked from head to toe, his erection hard and thick, tapping his belly. So absolutely perfect, he left her breathless.

"Come here," he whispered, stepping closer as she finally got rid of her panties.

Before she could even blink, he'd lifted her, bridal style, and settled her in the middle of the big bed. When he lay next to her and ran his hand slowly down her body, she gave up trying to catch her breath.

She knew he was about to wreck her, and she wanted that, craved it. And prayed that tonight wouldn't be the last time.

But it very well could be, because she had to tell him. "Um, I hate to say it but…condoms?"

Seth muttered a curse.

"Sorry."

He leaned in to kiss her, then making a supreme effort, he thrust himself out of bed. The moment he turned to rummage through his bag, Hannah dropped her head onto the pillow.

Tomorrow. She was going to tell him everything tomorrow. Right after the barbecue. No matter what she found out in the morning. Even if the whole plan fell apart, she still wanted him to know. Keeping it to herself might be technically fine, but it didn't feel right.

But for tonight? She wanted to enjoy him as if there

would be no tomorrow at all. And wake up to the man she cared for far more than was wise.

"WHAT THE HELL are you doing here? I didn't expect to see you." Clint walked out of the barn just as Seth got out of his truck.

"I figured I'd come help with the vaccinations and branding, then take the afternoon off."

His brother frowned. "I didn't know you'd be here, so I postponed it."

Seth sighed. He should've thought of that. They had enough new calves that the job would require all hands on deck. "I know you can still use my help."

"Well, sure, but what about Hannah? Doesn't she leave on Sunday?"

"She's got stuff to do. We'll meet up later." He hadn't come out and asked what she had going on. He assumed it had something to do with work. But since Hannah hadn't volunteered any details, he hadn't asked. His gaze was drawn to the house, then to the addition they used as an office. "You know if Dad's going to be around today?"

"He's home now. I don't know about later." Clint narrowed his eyes. "Don't tell me you're moving to Dallas. Is that what you want to tell him?"

Seth snorted a laugh. "No. You trying to get rid of me?"

Clint smiled. "Look, Hannah is great. If I didn't know better I would've guessed you two have been together for a couple years."

"I know." Seth had to agree. He'd never felt more comfortable with a woman before. "But we've only known each other for five days. So, no, I'm not moving to Dallas."

"Selfishly, I'm glad. It's been damn good to have you

around again. But I gotta admit, Lila and I started out the same way." Clint moved closer and lowered his voice. "This doesn't need to go any further, but I seriously gave some thought to moving to California if she wanted to live near her parents."

Well, that wouldn't be a problem with Hannah, Seth thought wryly. But what Clint had just admitted surprised him. "What made you stay?"

"It never became an issue. Now, to be clear, I wasn't looking forward to moving. But I would have for Lila."

"Interesting." Seth shrugged. "I'm never going to get to know Hannah well enough to be faced with that kind of decision, so moot point." He watched Joe lead a new colt toward the corral. "That little guy is really something," he said, nodding at the horse, but thinking only of Hannah.

Her infectious laugh. The way her eyes sparkled, excited or not. Her smart mouth…shit, no telling how often it got her into trouble. Though he wouldn't ever want to change that about her. He could even get used to her singing, if he had the chance.

"Hell, bro. You're screwed," Clint said, laughing.

Seth blinked. "What? I was admiring the colt."

"Right. Look, if you need to talk to Dad, I'd catch him now," Clint said, starting toward the stable. "Then get out of here. And for Christ's sake, get some sleep tonight."

Staring after his brother, Seth smiled a little and ran a hand through his uncombed hair. Clint was being a good sport. Of course, he always had been, even though most of the burden of the ranch had fallen on him at a fairly young age. Too young to shoulder the kind of responsibility he'd taken on without complaint.

Seth had been back for seven months, but it still stung to know his mom and Clint had suffered the brunt of Seth's long stretch of behaving like a prick. And yet they'd never stopped urging him to come home, so ready to forgive and forget.

He glanced again at the office that for many years had been his father's hideout. Torture chamber, more like it. Damn good cattleman. Terrible businessman. Now Clint and Seth were the only ones who used the office, so he wasn't sure why he was staring at it like his dad would suddenly materialize.

Yesterday, Hannah's question about whether the land purchase had anything to do with his return had forced him to do some thinking. No one had said anything at the time, but on some level he'd taken it as a sign that, after ten years, the family finally believed he'd straightened himself out. Especially after he'd dropped the bomb that he'd covered for Bobby.

Man, what a tough conversation that had been... *Oh, by the way, I shamed and disappointed you, not to mention costing you a small fortune, all for nothing, all because of a misguided sense of honor.* It still had the power to cripple him if he let himself dwell on it.

And now, he had to close the final chapter. He had honestly believed he was done. Thought there was nothing more to say. Any lingering hurt and resentment could be stuffed down deep enough it would eventually fade. But he'd been wrong.

He walked toward the house, hoping like hell he could catch his dad without being waylaid by his mom or Lila. He wanted this to be quick and private, preferably without anyone knowing they were talking behind a closed door. That alone would feed his mom's curiosity.

As soon as he opened the front door he saw his dad carrying a mug of coffee. From the time Seth was a small kid, his dad had drunk a whole pot every morning. Now it was half decaf, doctor's orders. "Hey, Pop."

"Hi, son. I didn't expect to see you today." He craned his neck, trying to see past Seth. "You alone?"

"Yep." Seth smiled at the stash of cookies his dad had almost hidden under a napkin. "So are you, I take it?"

"This little snack is gonna be our secret," his dad said. "No sense worrying your mom over it."

Seth followed him into the den. "Refresh my memory. Is cutting back on sugar the doctor's orders or Mom's?"

"Well, they're both pains in the ass about every little thing I eat." His father took the far side of the couch and set down his mug on the end table. "Come sit with me for a while. We never get any time alone."

Seth took a deep breath. His dad was probably going to wish it had stayed that way. "For the record," he said, taking a seat. "That's not a *little* snack." He put a hand up to forestall the inevitable grumbling. "I say that with love and concern. We'd all like to have you around for a good long while."

His dad stared back for a few seconds, then looked away to sip his coffee.

"You must be thinking I have a lot of nerve. Being as I was the one who caused most of your stress, and believe me—"

"Stop, son. I never thought that, even once, and I don't think it now. Someday you'll be a father and figure out it all comes with the job. The good, the bad and the ugly. Because, truth be told, as parents, sometimes we get it wrong."

Seth met his dad's eyes. It was as if he'd read his mind. It should've given him the final push he needed. Instead, he felt the urge to rethink his options. He stared at the family pictures on the mantel. Hannah was right. He was lucky to have his family…to have *this* family. Goddamn it. Maybe this wasn't the time to bring it up. Maybe the past was the past and his feelings should stay buried.

"Just go ahead and speak your mind, Seth. I'm listening." His dad's tone of voice was as kind as his eyes. "We've come too far for either of us to hold anything back now."

Seth cleared his throat. "I thought I knew how to say this, at least without coming off like a jackass. It's about that night I got arrested—" Pausing, he took a breath. "Why did you leave me in jail, Pop? I could've been out in an hour, but you left me sweating in that cell for the whole weekend."

His dad lowered his gaze, nodding slowly.

"I know it wasn't a matter of raising bail. Sheriff Gladstone released me on your promise I'd show up in court. And I get that you wanted to teach me a lesson. I do." Seth was unprepared for the old anger and hurt that flared inside him. "But it wasn't as if I'd been in trouble before. A few missed curfews and stuff, but nothing big."

"I've thought about that myself, many times," his father admitted. "The simple answer is that I was wrong and I later regretted it. By Saturday night your mom was begging me to get you out. Swore she'd never speak to me again if I didn't. She made good on the threat for over a week, too."

Seth waited for him to say more. "So, that's it? You were wrong?"

His father frowned. "I'm not sure what it is you're asking."

Seth needed to watch his tone. He wasn't looking for a fight. "You said that was the simple answer. I just wanted…" He exhaled sharply. "You *never* would have done that to Nathan or Clint, Dad."

The room got quiet.

His father furrowed his brow as if he didn't understand or he was trying to decide how to respond.

"I always got good grades. I didn't smoke or use drugs or drink. Well, I did drink beer a few times at parties." A fact he hadn't hidden from his parents. "And I'm not saying Nathan and Clint did any of those things. I just don't get it. Was I too interested in astronomy and science? Did I not pay enough attention to what needed doing here? Tell me. I'm not pointing fingers or looking for excuses. I just want to know how I disappointed you so much."

His father looked stricken.

Seth sighed and rubbed the tension in his neck. "I shouldn't have brought it up. It's all water under the bridge."

"You never disappointed me, Seth. Well, except for that one time, of course. But I think I was more shocked than anything. And you're right. I doubt I would've left Nathan or Clint locked up that long. Probably overnight, though," he said, thoughtfully. "Now, please don't mistake what I'm about to say, because your brothers weren't bad kids. But they pulled their share of crazy stunts.

"If I'd gotten a call to bail out either of them, I would've been angry and disappointed, and they would've suffered some serious consequences. But I'm not sure it would've surprised me all that much."

Seth smiled a little at that. "Are you serious?"

"Yes, I'm serious, and you don't need to repeat any of this.

"Of you three boys, your mom and I always knew that you'd be the one to finish college and go on to do great things. Every teacher you ever had couldn't stop talking about how bright you were and eager to learn. Shoot, we already knew that.

"Don't get me wrong, your brothers have smarts. Hell,

if it weren't for Clint taking over the books, the bank would probably own the Whispering Pines by now. And look at Nathan. Can't argue with his success. But those two are more like your old man. Peel everything away and we're cowpokes at heart. Not you, Seth. You've got something special. And the truth is, you had me stumped. I didn't know what to do. I kept thinking every move was the wrong one and spent the whole weekend second-guessing myself."

Seth swallowed around the lump in his throat. His dad had hit the nail on the head. Deep down, Seth had felt he didn't belong. Nathan and Clint were cut from the same cloth as their dad. They made him proud. "I figured I was the black sheep."

"No, son, like your mom always said, you're the shining star of the family. The crown jewel…or something like that."

"More like the son who caused you the most grief."

His dad grinned. "That's what they call ironic, isn't it?"

Seth laughed, feeling as if a load had been lifted.

"Hey, you want one of these oatmeal cookies?" His father lifted the napkin. "They're real good. Your mom made them last night."

"You realize she probably counted them before she left."

His father's jaw went slack. "Hell, I bet you're right. Oh, well, since you're here I'll just blame it on you."

_18_

SETH ARRIVED AT the Sundance in the mood for a barbecue.

After he parked, he called Hannah's cell. He wanted a few minutes alone with her, if she could swing it.

He hadn't decided if he'd tell her what had happened with his dad, but he doubted he would, even though he was well aware she'd played a part in him having the guts to bare his soul.

"Where are you?" she asked the second she answered.

"Sundance. Parked by the stable. Can you sneak away? I was thinking of getting you in my truck and making out a little."

"I'll be right there."

He hung up, then put down the windows just enough to let in the evening breeze. Thought about turning the key, playing some nice background music. Instead, he just kept an eye out, and before he knew it, the passenger door opened, and Hannah, looking pretty in a green sundress and sandals, climbed in.

"Hey, hot stuff. Heard you were looking for a good time."

"Lucky for me, I've already got the perfect date right next to me."

She leaned over the console, and he met her halfway. The kiss started out tame but turned steamy fast. At least this time they wouldn't fog the windows.

When they finally came up for air, she looked at him as if she hadn't seen him in days. "I'm so glad you're here."

He took a good look at her, too. "Is something wrong? Your eyes are a little red."

"Allergies," she said with a dismissive wave. "Did you have something you wanted to tell me?"

"I just wanted to see you before I had to be on my best behavior."

"Oh, you don't have to worry about that. In fact, I was hoping you'd do just the opposite."

"Okay. I think."

Her eyes widened with excitement as she laid out a pretty devious little plan having to do with a couple of Sundance guests who'd not been very nice.

"So when I give you the signal," she said, grinning with such a wicked gleam he thought he should probably be worried, "look all sexy and hot, and put your arm around my shoulders. Maybe nibble on my neck or something."

He couldn't help but laugh. "You're serious?"

"Course I am."

Of course she was. "That's all fine, but how exactly am I supposed to look all sexy and hot?"

She squeezed his arm. "You don't even have to try."

"Right. Like when you made me turn over last night because I was snoring too loud?"

"Even then. Besides, you only did that for a minute. Anyway," she said, her cheeks a delicate pink, "it's only if those two mean girls end up staying to eat. Hopefully, they'll have hooked up with some unsuspecting cowboys for the night."

He looked at the parking area in front of the house. "Doesn't look like too many people are here yet."

"Rachel said it isn't a big deal. They have a barbecue once a week for the guests. But Cole and Jamie will be here, and Jesse and his wife. Matt's coming, although he doesn't usually. I'm not sure about Nikki and Trace. It's all casual. You know, beers and beef."

"Okay, then. We might as well get started. I've got to practice my sexy walk."

She grabbed his hand, and they headed toward the picnic tables out by the aspens. Two of the long tables had already been set up with plates, silverware, condiments and glasses, and there was a big ice chest filled with sodas and beer near the buffet table.

Hannah's cell beeped and she pulled it out to read the text. "Oh, crap. Rachel needs me in the kitchen. I'm sorry. Can you go do cowboy things for a little while?"

"As soon as I figure out what that is, I will do just that."

She kissed him. "Thank you. I'll try not to be too long."

"Wait." He caught her arm. "Are you sure nothing's wrong?"

"Positive."

Well, *he* wasn't, he thought as he watched her head across the yard.

"Landers. Over here."

It had been a while since he'd seen Jesse McAllister, who was standing with his brother Cole. They'd all known each other since they were kids. The two of them were Nathan and Clint's ages, and they'd all played high school football together until a huge county dispute put the Whispering Pines in Twin Creeks' territory.

He walked by the ice chest and grabbed a cold one before he met up with the two men.

"Hey, your timing is perfect," Cole said, with a quick glance to the left. "The guests are on the prowl, so you'd better make it clear real quick that you're spoken for."

"I have my instructions," he said, lifting his beer. "Good to see you, Jesse. It's been too long."

"That it has. Hey, I heard you did some time in the air force, too."

"Yep, but I wasn't a glorified pilot."

Jesse laughed. "Shit. I flew cargo. You're thinking of the fighter jocks."

Seth smiled, then noticed the herd of guests had swung their way.

"Don't say I didn't warn you." Cole took a swig from his bottle. A gold band gleamed on his ring finger.

"Hey, I heard you both married Sundance guests. Is that true?"

Jesse grinned. "You got us there."

Seth figured he had about twenty seconds before the women ganged up on them. "How did that work out? I mean, you must've done the long distance thing before your wives moved here, right?"

The brothers had matching raised eyebrows. The amused grins came next. "Any particular reason you want to know?" Jesse asked.

Seth's window of opportunity was just about to close. "Fuck you guys."

The three of them laughed.

"You're on vacation," Mrs. McAllister said, as she passed through the kitchen with a pitcher of margaritas. "Don't let Rachel make you work for your supper."

Hannah grinned. "Yeah, Rachel, listen to your mom."

"Why don't you just sing us a song while I finish getting the corn ready?"

"Ha. Very funny." Sitting at the table, Hannah continued to tear pieces of tinfoil to wrap the corn. She'd started out on the counter but working on the beautiful pearl-gray granite countertop felt so wrong. Her gaze wandered over to the high-end stainless steel appliances. This certainly wasn't the type of ranch kitchen she'd grown up with.

Hilda was at the stove, and so was Jamie, who'd given her a hug when she'd walked in.

They didn't really need Hannah's help at this point, and she thought about going to find Seth. But when she'd looked out the window and seen him talking with Cole and Jesse, she decided to hang with Rachel for a while.

It didn't take long before the last of the food preparations were done, but Rachel held Hannah back when Hilda and Jamie left with their trays. "You want a beer?"

Hannah nodded.

After getting a couple of bottles from the fridge, Rachel led her out of the kitchen to the family room. "I've been so busy with the guests we've barely seen each other. I think Seth won't miss you too much for the next little while."

Hannah grabbed her beer and sank into an overstuffed chair, grateful to have a few minutes alone with her friend. The day had been…challenging.

"So," Rachel said, making herself comfortable across from Hannah. "Why do I have the feeling something's going on with you?"

"What do you mean?"

"You've had this look on your face. It reminded me a lot of the nights before finals. Has something happened? I hope you aren't letting that idiot Jasper get to you."

"Why? Is he spreading more bullshit about me?"

"Oh, he's a pain in everyone's ass. He's got the whole town crazy. There was a fight at the Watering Hole last night, and that hasn't happened in ages."

Hannah's good mood—which had been precarious to begin with, knowing the discussion she and Seth were having later—vanished. "I'm sure my name's come up about a hundred times."

"Oh, don't worry about that. He's got enough locals to pick on."

Which probably meant Seth. Hannah had made him a target ten minutes after the meeting had ended. Probably before that. She lowered her head, hunching forward, her hands gripping her beer between her knees.

"Hey, what the heck's going on?" Rachel sounded worried now.

"I don't know how this has become so complicated," Hannah said. "Look, you remember I told you how bad things had gotten on my dad's ranch, right?"

"Yeah."

"Well, when I heard about the grazing permits, it seemed like that might be a way for them to get back on track. You know, truck the cattle up to Montana, let them get fat and increase the herd."

Rachel was so quiet, Hannah had to look up. The moment she saw her friend's expression, she wished she hadn't.

"That's why you were at the meeting," Rachel said, her voice very different from just a moment before. "Why you were asking those questions."

"Yeah. Kind of."

"And?"

"It could work. I'm not sure my father will agree, but at least he'd have the option. I just wish I'd understood what I was getting into."

"Hannah, have you talked this over with Seth?"

She wanted to cry. Just burst into tears at her own foolishness. Why had she waited so long to talk to him? "He doesn't know."

"Shit. Well, that's not good." Rachel stood up. Walked the length of the room, drank some, walked back over to the other chair. "You should have said something sooner. But that's done and gone. The truth is, no matter what, Seth is going to understand that you're trying to save the family ranch."

"I don't know what he's going to think of me." She looked up. "I know you guys don't need grazing land, but I could tell even you were upset a minute ago."

"I wasn't upset. Surprised, maybe. Look, Seth will come around, but you have to tell him. It's only fair. Now, don't *you* get all upset. Listen to me. My brothers were absolutely appalled when I suggested we use part of the Sundance as a dude ranch. They were furious with me. Hated the idea. Then, when they finally, grudgingly, agreed that it would help us get through the recession, the town got wind and they all went nuts. No one wanted it.

"And then, just last year, Sadie agreed to have a movie company come and use the town as a set for their film. Talk about an uproar. My God, there wasn't a soul who didn't have some kind of opinion worth fighting over. But the money that movie brought to Blackfoot Falls made a huge difference. Even a few old shops reopened.

"You do what you have to do to save your ranch. To save a town. A community. No one, especially in cowboy country, likes change. You should have heard the outcry when the Circle K started using ATVs instead of horses. You'd have thought it was the start of the apocalypse. Unfortunately, you'll be the first outsider bringing cattle into the area, so there will be some…bumps. So after you and Seth have dinner, you take him somewhere private and you tell him. Everything. Honestly, there was no way you could have known about the hoopla going on right now, and you'd just met Seth, so you couldn't have known about his history with Jasper. But you do now. So tell him. He's a good guy, Hannah."

"I agree. He is. But I'm not sure this is something he should forgive. I appreciate you talking to me. So much. It's made a few things real clear. First of all, I'm not coming back to the Sundance."

"What?"

"I've extended my stay in town. I can't let people think your family is siding with me on this. And I have to distance myself from Seth, too. He deserves that."

"Why don't you let us decide what we need to do? Anyway, most of the crap going on has nothing to do with grazing permits. Some of the ranchers will use any excuse to gain supporters to go against the government."

Hannah stood up. In her case, that didn't matter. It was about lying to Seth while knowing what he'd gone through to make up past wrongs that had hurt his family. "I swear, if I could do it again, I'd never even give grazing permits a second thought. In fact, I hope it all falls apart."

"I don't think you believe that. Not if it can save your folks so much misery."

Sighing, Hannah shook her head. "As bad as I am a singer, I'm a worse actress. And now I've got to go join the party and act like everything's just peachy."

Rachel rose and pulled her into a hug. "You can do this. You can do anything. You're my fearless friend. And you're a good daughter. Don't let your father convince you otherwise. Now let's go have a barbecue."

SETH OPENED THE passenger door, but before Hannah could climb in, he caught her around the waist. "Not so fast," he said, trapping her between his body and the truck seat. "I've waited too long to get you alone."

Hannah turned to face him and arched back when he tried to swoop in for a kiss. "People can still see us, you know."

"So? Think I care that you're a government spy?"

Oh, God.

She tried not to whimper.

Nerves and fear were mixing in her stomach. Good thing she hadn't eaten much. How could she have lived in denial for this long? The reason she hadn't already explained to Seth about her big plan was because she knew it might upset him, that it could ruin their week together. At the same time, she'd convinced herself it wouldn't matter to him so why bring it up?

Seeing the look on Rachel's face, hearing the change in her voice…what an eye-opener. Hannah firmly believed Rachel didn't care about grazing permits, and yet…it would be the same with Seth. Only worse, because Hannah should've told him.

He leaned back, searching her face. "What's wrong? You've been edgy all evening."

"I don't know, I just—" She forced a smile, then pressed a kiss to his lips. "I have to tell you something that I'm dreading like crazy."

"Okay." He moved back a step. "We should probably get in the truck first."

"I think so." The second she was seated she thought of her rental, parked two cars over. Her luggage already stored in the trunk. "Don't forget I drove separately."

"Ah, right. Let's talk, then we'll figure it out."

She nodded and watched him walk around the hood.

Even in the dim light she could see the concern in his face. Had he overheard something? No, he'd been in a great mood until a moment ago.

He slid behind the wheel and looked at her. "The three extra vacation days you got. Did your boss renege?"

"Oh, no, it's nothing like that." That news she probably could've handled much better.

The oddest smile tugged at his mouth. "I happen to have some experience with bottling things up. Believe me when I tell you it's better to just let it out."

Hannah nodded. "Okay. Well, I know you're aware of the drought in Texas. Other states are having problems too, of course." She realized she was picking at her fingernails and stopped. Taking a deep breath, she said, "I told my dad he should buy a grazing permit and ship his cattle here."

Seth's brows went up. "Wow. That's—there's a lot to consider. The initial expense can be sizeable, and it's not easy crossing state lines—"

"I know."

"You do?"

She gave up trying to swallow and nodded.

"Sherwood?"

"Mostly from my own research, but yes, he gave me information, too."

A muscle worked in his jaw. "How long have you known you wanted to do this?"

She stared down at her hands. "Not long."

"You told me you didn't know anything about grazing permits."

At his cool tone, nausea churned in her stomach. "I didn't, not until I started asking about it. We saw the sign for the town meeting that first night, remember?"

"And you didn't think to tell me about your plans?"

"Your family doesn't need BLM land, so I didn't think it mattered... No, you're right. I'm making excuses because I screwed up and I..." Her mouth stopped working.

"Hannah, you're a smart woman. You have to know it's not about the land or whose herd is grazing where. I told you I didn't want to get involved."

"Right, and that's partly why I didn't tell you—" Between the anger and hurt on his face and the sound of her feeble excuses she wanted to curl up and die.

"So, you knew before we went to the meeting. That's why the questions. Later I asked you why you were taking notes and you lied." Seth sighed. "The meeting with Sherwood..."

"No, that was accidental." When had she become such a damn coward? "I didn't tell you because I didn't want you to hate me, and that's the truth. But now you probably do hate me and I don't blame you."

"Or maybe you just wanted to keep me on the hook so you'd have a playmate for the week."

"Seth, please, you don't believe that."

"Goddamn it, Hannah." He shoved a hand through his hair, his expression a complete wreck. "I laid it all out for you. How I'd let my family down. I told you how it had taken me ten goddamn years to make things right. Jesus, you knew my past with Jasper. You didn't think I would've cared about getting involved with him in any way? Or making my family a target? Because you weren't exactly an innocent bystander like I was telling people, now were you? And there's a whole lot of ways someone can spin my association with you."

She couldn't speak at first. "I'm sorry. So very, very sorry." She struggled to recall the advice Rachel had given her. Mostly she drew a blank. "Honestly, all I could think about was helping my dad save his ranch."

"You don't even like the man."

"That's true," she whispered.

"So what am I supposed to think about your feelings for me?" He snorted, shaking his head. "Right. Vacation playmate. I forgot."

Hannah flinched. "You're angry. Of course you are, but after you calm down I hope you realize that isn't anything close to how I feel about you."

She wasn't sure he was even listening, or had heard a word she'd said. He just stared out into the darkness, the muscle working in his jaw.

"I left my family open to gossip because of you. It doesn't matter if the rumors are true or not, you know how that works. And the real kicker, if you'd been honest with me from the beginning, I would've defended you. Hell, I would've helped you figure out if it was feasible to bring the herd. But you blindsided me, and now I can't even defend myself. Not after Jasper gets wind of this."

"I'll make sure he understands I hid everything from you," Hannah said, wanting desperately to take his hand, but she didn't dare. "I'll make sure everyone knows. Even if I have to take an ad out in the *Gazette*."

Seth just shook his head.

"I've checked out of the Sundance and moved my things to my car. I'm going to be staying at the motel. Try to put some distance between me and the McAllisters. And—" She cleared her throat. "And you. I'm assuming that's what you want."

His reply was nothing but tension-charged silence that threatened to smother her.

"I'll hang on to your clothes and toiletries until you come by the room. Unless you want to handle it differently."

"So, this deal is a sure thing?"

Head down, she nodded. "Yeah, pretty much."

Seth let out a humorless laugh. "You're trying to please the man at all costs. Hope it ends up worth it."

"I'm trying to help him save the—" Indignation died on her lips. That was a lie, too. Her motives had little to do with saving the ranch.

He put the key in the ignition and started the truck. It was her cue to get out.

Hannah hesitated. But did she really have anything left to say that wouldn't just make him hate her more? "Sorry" didn't seem nearly enough.

She got out and walked to her car without looking back.

"Hannah Elizabeth, I understand you're upset, but there's no call for you to use that kind of language."

"I have to talk to him today. I've already extended my vacation so I can take care of things on this end."

After a brief silence, her mom said, "Well, I don't know what to tell you. I can't force him to come inside. It's hard for him to accept your help. You know as well as I do he's a proud man."

Hannah slumped. Had she really expected anything different? "Then tell me this—what exactly is he proud of?"

Her mom didn't answer.

"No, really, I'd like to know. Proud of verbally abusing you for years? And me. That is, when he wasn't outright ignoring my existence."

"Hannah, please."

"I'm not blaming you, Mom," Hannah said, though she did think some of it was her mom's fault. "Actually, we don't need to talk. Just tell him it's not going to work."

"Hannah, don't."

"I have to go, Mom. I really do."

She disconnected and gave in to a good hard cry.

HE HATED STACKING HAY, but it was that or punch his fist through a wall.

Seth had slept like crap, his mind going over and over what Hannah had told him. It felt more like a nightmare than something real. Especially because he couldn't even remember everything they'd said.

All he knew for sure was that Hannah had gone behind his back and made plans that would make him look like a fool and put his innocent family directly in the line of fire.

He picked up another sixty-pound bale, feeling the burn as he hauled it to the stack.

Just when he'd made things right with his dad, she had to do something that would cause no end of grief. Jasper would be in his glory, and Seth could only imagine what it would be like to go into Blackfoot Falls now. Jesus.

He'd deliberately pointed out that Hannah was visiting, only here for a week, so why in hell would she care about grazing permits? He'd thought it was the truth.

Shit. He'd never imagined for a second that Hannah of all people would screw him like that. He'd clicked with her from that first minute. It was as if they'd known each other for years instead of days, and the thought of her going back to Texas had made him sick. Like losing his best friend.

But he'd obviously gotten things wrong. Believing her had been easy, and he hated to think she'd played him, but it sure looked like it. If only she'd talked to him. All of this could have been avoided. He'd still be the target of gossip, but he wouldn't look like a liar and a traitor. He figured it would take about a day for everyone to start claiming he was a government spy along with Hannah.

And his family…shit. They'd hear about this for years to come, and it would be his fault.

Wiping the sweat from his brow, he almost bumped into Clint.

"What are you doing here?" His brother looked at him as if he was loco. "I figured you wouldn't be back until tomorrow. Isn't Hannah leaving soon?"

"I don't know. I think she's staying a few more days."

"Whoa, what the hell happened?"

Seth hooked another bale and practically dislocated his shoulders lifting it so hard.

"Okay," Clint said. "If you're stacking hay, something's going on. Just know if you need to talk, I'm here."

By the time Seth had put the new bale on the stack, Clint had disappeared.

Turning to do the next round, Seth's eyes went to the spot where Hannah had been standing when she'd gotten that phone call from her father. Remembering how she'd physically changed the moment she'd heard his voice shifted something inside him.

As he slowed his breathing, he played out the scene in his head, not once, but twice. Recalling what he'd thought at the time. How she probably didn't even realize how her body became submissive, how her voice thinned. There was some messed-up stuff going on with that relationship.

Something he was more than a little familiar with.

Goddamn it. He'd never been the type to kick someone while they were down, and he wasn't about to start now. Not with Hannah.

God, never Hannah.

HANNAH GLANCED AROUND the room. Luckily, she'd left most of her things in the trunk last night. Clearly some part of her knew it would turn out like this.

She'd already changed her flight, and she had plenty of time to drive to Kalispell, but she wasn't sure about what to do with Seth's things. She was thinking seriously about using them to force him to talk to her, but hadn't she done enough damage?

Oh, Lord. She could not start crying again.

Thinking she heard a knock she looked out the peephole then opened the door. Seth was standing there. He looked so very tired.

"I guess you want your things," she mumbled, and

stepped back. "I know I have no right to ask, but could we talk, just for five minutes?"

He eyed her overnight bag sitting on the bed and nodded.

"First, we're not bringing any cattle. The matter is closed."

"What's your dad going to do?"

"Whatever he wants. I don't care."

"Why? You went through a lot of trouble."

"More like I caused a lot of trouble." She swallowed a lump of tears, then turned away to blink more from her eyes.

"I'm never going to please my dad and I think I've finally made peace with that. But mostly, I won't risk hurting you or your family or the McAllisters. You're the most amazing people I've ever met. You've all treated me better than—"

"Listen, you do what you have to do and don't worry about any of us."

She didn't know what surprised her more, his words or that he almost touched her. "That's exactly what I'm doing. I refuse to hurt any one of you."

Seth studied her face a moment. "I was angry. I said angry things. But the bottom line is that my family and me, and I'm pretty sure the McAllisters, we'd all support any decision you make. All of us understand the importance of family."

Hannah was glad someone did. Her tongue felt dry and thick. "I wasn't trying to save the ranch. That was a lie, too, though it wasn't intentional," she whispered. "I just wanted him to love me."

Humiliated beyond belief at the truth she'd been unwilling to face, the tears flowed and there wasn't a damn thing she could do about it but hide. She tried to beeline it to the bathroom, but he caught her wrist and pulled her into his arms.

"Let me finish, huh?"

Burying her face against his chest, she nodded.

"That you even considered my family's feelings and were willing to make a sacrifice to keep them out of it means a lot to me." Seth paused and she could feel a slight tremor in his body. "*You* mean a lot to me. That you feel you have to win your dad's love? I don't know what to say to that, sweetheart. The whole idea is inconceivable to me. But I guess it would be, since I find it impossible not to love you."

Hannah's cheek was pressed against him. She thought she heard right, but she'd been sniffling and crying, and if she got it wrong she would just die for sure. His heartbeat was strong and steady, and shouldn't it be going crazy if he'd said what she thought he did?

"Hey." Seth hugged her a little tighter. "It's your turn to talk."

That made her smile. She swallowed thickly and looked up at him. "Could you repeat that thing you said before? Just so I don't embarrass myself."

He smiled and drew the pad of his thumb gently across her cheek. "How about you just tell me the truth?"

She swallowed again. "I love you, Seth," she said, meeting his eyes. Then an amazing thing happened— her heart began to slow. It was certainty that kept the beat steady, she realized. Steady and slow. "I love you so much."

"Ah, Hannah." He tightened his arms around her. "I'm glad it wasn't just me. I knew we had something real between us by the third day. It was crazy and hard to believe." He leaned back and locked gazes with her.

"We have some talking to do. But just know that I'm willing to do whatever it takes to keep this love strong."

Hannah saw the truth in his darkened eyes. "I can't think of anything I'd like better," she whispered and hugged him as tight as she could.

Seth smiled. "I can think of one thing that might come close."

She laughed. "It wouldn't have anything to do with getting naked, would it?"

"See what I mean? We're like two peas in a pod." He smiled at her eye-roll, then kissed her. "I love you, baby," he murmured against her mouth. "With all my heart."

Hannah felt a fresh round of tears well and prayed they wouldn't fall. Happy tears, but still.

And hiccups. God, please, no hiccups. Although she had the cure right here in her arms. The cure for so many things she couldn't begin to count. "I love you too, Seth Landers."

* * * * *

Get 2 Free Books,
Plus 2 Free Gifts—
just for trying the Reader Service!

"We have one minute," he heard his commander say
through his helmet's speakers. "Is your captain ready?
Over?"

"She will be," Dylan answered. He slung an arm over
a rope line and held fast when another swell lifted him
off his feet. The ship groaned as sheets of metal strained
against each other like fault lines before an earthquake.
The lashings clanked. "Send down the strop. Over."

"You have fifty seconds and then I want you on deck,
Holt," barked his commander.

Dylan shoved his way along the slick deck, propelling
himself across its steep slant. "Roger that."

He would get Nolee out. End of story.

Descending as fast as he dared, he fought the wind
and dropped down into the hull again. Icy water made his
breath catch even with the benefit of the dry suit. Nolee
should have been out of here long before now.

"I've almost got it." Her strained voice emerged from blue lips. Her movements were jerky as she twisted wire around the still gushing pipe. She was losing motor function. Hypothermia was already setting in.

"It's over, Nolee. Come with me now."

When she opened her mouth, her head lolled. Her eyelids dropped. Reacting on instinct, he grabbed her limp form before she crumpled into the freezing water.

He hauled her out of the hull and across the deck where a rescue strop dangled. Damn, damn, damn. His hands weren't cooperating, his own motor function feeling the effects of the cold. Once he'd tethered them together, he gave his flight mechanic a thumbs-up. The boat flung them sideways, careening over the rail.

Swinging, their feet skimmed the deadly swells. The line jerked them up through the stinging air. He tightened his arms around her. With only a tether connecting her to him, he couldn't lose his grip.

As they rose, he forced himself not to look at her. He'd dreamed about that face too many times, even after he left Kodiak to forget her.

But he wouldn't be doing his job if he didn't hold her close. And heaven help him—no matter how much she'd gutted him nine years ago—he couldn't deny she felt damned good in his arms.

Don't miss
HIS LAST DEFENSE by Karen Rock,
available April 2017 wherever
Harlequin® Blaze® books and ebooks are sold.

www.Harlequin.com

Love the Harlequin book you just read?

Your opinion matters.

Review this book on your favorite book site, review site, blog or your own social media properties and share your opinion with other readers!

Be sure to connect with us at:
Harlequin.com/Newsletters
Facebook.com/HarlequinBooks
Twitter.com/HarlequinBooks

HREVIEWS